WORTH THE RISK

BEA BORGES

WORTH THE RISK

BEA BORGES

ISBN: 979-8-89443-619-7

Cover Design: Summer Grove- @summerrgrove
Formatting: Robert Harrison- Seneca Author Services

This is for the anxious girls, the ones who worry.
You're so worthy of love.
Don't let your anxiety tell you different.

XO, Bea

RHETT

The ticking of the clock hand and my steady breathing are the only sounds I've heard for the past hour. I'm alone in a bright white room, staring blankly at the tiles of the ceiling. The last few years I've lived my dream of playing hockey at a professional level. I have gotten to do something I love and make a career out of it when most people never even get that chance. So, even though I'm lying on an exam table with the torn ligaments in my knee repaired (but not the same and with no hope of playing professional hockey again) I remind myself to be grateful for the opportunity I was so fortunate to have. There's a lot I'm going to miss about this chapter in my life but there's a lot I'm looking forward to.

I have other dreams and aspirations for my life. I've watched so many of my friends get married and settle down and it's made me think about her on more than one occasion. I've thought about our time together a lot over the last eight years. It's the small things that seem to bring on the strongest memories. She's in the fresh baked goods I get at the market on Saturdays and the notebooks I buy, but never write in. She's in the books I pick up but never open. They just sit on my shelves collecting dust.

I have gone on plenty of dates over the years and have been with other women. Only to reach the same conclusion eventually. There was always going to be the morning after. Even if it wasn't exactly *'the morning after'*. There was always going to be the moment where I had thought that maybe this time it would be different, but it wasn't.

Unfortunately, this earned me a bit of a reputation. Most of the guys on the team and the women I had been with thought my not calling them or sneaking out was because I had gotten what I wanted and couldn't be bothered to stick around. It wasn't like I had set out to hurt anyone, but when I looked over at the woman I was sitting across from at dinner or when they were lying next to me, there was the dreadful moment I knew it wasn't going anywhere.

The last time that happened was two years ago. That's when I decided to solely focus on hockey. I had just seen her at a game with my family. The way she had jumped into my arms and hugged me after I came out of the locker room. I never wanted to let her go.

All the feelings I had been trying to replicate with someone else were so easily felt in that moment. That night we talked like we hadn't in years. Like no time had passed. I thought maybe there was a shot at being with her again. When she didn't answer my call the next day or come to my next game with everyone, I figured she didn't feel the same way.

Now, I'm on my way back home to Silverthorne, Colorado

to accept the job I've been offered as the new High School hockey coach. Along with getting to be with my family more and hopefully coaching my new team to victory, maybe I'll be able to find out why Winslow Parker ended things with me the summer before our lives went in different directions.

WINNIE

"He did not say that!"

I'm driving the two and a half hours it takes to get from Palisade to Silverthorne, the smell of eggplant parmesan and garlic bread keeping me company. I should probably be crying over the events of the last four hours, but when I think about it too long, I can't stop myself from laughing. That should clue you in on how I decide to deal with things in my life. I find the humor or completely avoid it at all costs. There is no in between. I went to Palisade to surprise my boyfriend of six months with his favorite dinner as a romantic gesture. However, after I arrived at his peach orchard and let myself into his home with the key he gave me last month, it became clear it was me that would be getting surprised.

"Win, tell me he did not say that!" my best friend Marigold gasps at me through my car's speaker. I called her when I was about 30 minutes from home, because I knew she would want to hear how tonight went. She wasn't prepared for this.

"He really did though. He also said that if I had been more 'emotionally available', he wouldn't have had to find someone else to 'take care of him'". She makes a gagging sound and I start laughing.

"Stop or I'm going to be sick—and where was she? Just standing there? The whole time?" I cringe, remembering the beautiful redhead with legs for days.

"Yes, she was definitely there for the whole show. She was also in one of his button downs." I sigh and try to sober my laughing. "She was just standing in his kitchen while he tried to explain that it didn't really mean anything."

"No. Winnie. No."

"Uh huh. I was almost more embarrassed for her than I was for me."

"What the hell do you have to be embarrassed about? He's the one that should be embarrassed!" Marigold is fiercely protective and for some reason finds all my quirks and issues charming where most people would find them exhausting. I find them exhausting.

"You're right. I'm not really embarrassed about what he did. I'm just not sure what to feel. I've never been cheated on before."

"Are you okay? Do you need me to come over when you get home?" I think about that. I should need a friend to comfort me, with ice cream and reality TV, but I don't. I'm...fine.

"Honestly, I think I'm okay. I know I shouldn't be, but I don't think he was completely wrong about me. I don't know if I'll ever be emotionally available."

"Winnie..." I head her off before she starts to hype me up.

"Seriously, Mare. I'm fine. A little anxious but fine. I think I'll stop by the bakery and check on Anna. I need to make sure things are set for this weekend anyway." She blows out a breath.

"You need to get some rest before the festival. You've been working every day at the bakery since before you even opened." Her tone is only reproachful.

"I will. Things will slow down after the weekend and as crazy as it sounds, being there will help me process. I always think better when I'm busy with my hands."

"That's not crazy, Win. It's how you're wired." Marigold Levinson is an absolute gem. A true treasure. She validates my feelings and encourages me to find outlets for my anxiety. I would take a bullet for her. I also have the knowledge that she would be able to save me. Did I mention she's a kick ass surgeon?

"Thank you. Love you. I'll call you tomorrow."

"Love you, too. Call me if you need me. I'm on call tonight but can be over in 10 minutes flat."

"I will. Get some sleep while you can. Night."

"Night, Win." I drive the rest of the way home, admiring my town as I go.

My bakery, Thistle and Sage, opened three months ago and tonight is the first night I had tried to take off from work. It didn't exactly go as planned. Anna, the sweet girl I hired to help me has been doing a great job. I left her in charge by herself tonight and although I'm sure she's doing great, I want to stop by and check. She just turned 18 and spends a lot of time on social media. She's also fantastic with customers.

After parking my car at home and walking the few blocks there, I push through the door.

"Winnie!?" I hear Anna from behind the counter. "I thought you wouldn't be in tonight. Aren't you supposed to be having a nice dinner with your boyfriend?" I cringe, because although I think getting over Sam isn't going to be an issue, I'm not looking forward to telling everyone who asks that we've broken up. Maybe I'll just let it go for tonight.

"I was but something came up..." Like catching him cheating on me. "...and we had to cancel." The entire relationship. "I thought I'd come in and get started on some of the dough for tomorrow and a couple things for the weekend. How's it going tonight?"

"Aww, I'm sorry. I know you were looking forward to the night off." I smile. "Everything here has been good! We sold out of most pastries by 6 but I stayed open just in case anyone wanted a coffee or one of the breads." She looks pleased with herself and it's nice to see her confidence growing.

"That's great. Sounds like you had everything covered. Thanks, Anna."

"Anytime! I'll start sweeping soon and let me know if there's anything else I can do." I smile at her and walk through the swinging door to the kitchen. As soon as I'm back there I take a deep breath. Today and the many days before are catching up to me. I can feel the fatigue settling in. That's why I like to keep moving. I don't like to dwell on negative feelings or emotions for too long.

I take a second to look around me. I love this kitchen. I may be exhausted but I'm also happy. The work and dedication I've put into Thistle and Sage is already paying off. I want to jump up and down but my muscles protest and cry out for rest. I feel older than I am tonight. At 30, 31 next week, I know I'm still young. Only sometimes I think my anxiety takes an extra toll.

I go long stretches where I feel more carefree, able to handle typical stresses and obstacles life throws my way, but then I'll get the pit in my stomach again. I never know when it will rear its ugly head. The nausea and headaches, the soreness and bone deep tiredness. Anxiety is something I will have to battle the rest of my life but with the help of my friends and family, an incredibly supportive community, and a therapist to help me work through bad episodes, my anxiety has become manageable and less frequent. I tune out my inner thoughts and try to focus on the bread I'm about to bake.

I work my way around the kitchen collecting and measuring ingredients. Instead of letting my thoughts drift back to the day I've had, I focus on the task at hand. I've loved being in the kitchen from a very young age. Colt and I moved to Silverthorne to live with Uncle Buck, my mother's brother, when I was 13, after losing our parents in a car accident.

I used to cook and bake with my mother every day. Whether we were preparing dinner or making something special, I spent so much of my time with her in the kitchen. I smile thinking of her, I don't allow myself this very often. It tends to make me sad and I don't do well with sad. Her sweet smile has faded in my mind over time. Slipping through my fingers like the flour I'm sifting. We were so young when it happened and relocated so quickly that I didn't think to ask for pictures or many keepsakes. I feel a tightness in my chest and rub at it, trying to clear it away, but only leaving flour and dough on my apron. Today has been more than enough, I don't need to add anything else on top of it.

I section my dough and put each one into baking tins. After I slide them into the drawer, I decide I had better start cleaning up around here. The end of summer festival is this weekend and I'm excited to be featured at a booth. This community has always been special. There's always an outreach or festival happening at least once a month.

Ding! I hear the door chime from the back room. I look at the big mounted clock and do a double take and groan. It's already 8:30.

"Hey, Anna! Could you please lock the door and flip the sign?" I ask. I guess she must have forgotten to lock up earlier.

I hear voices out front and I'm hoping no one is looking to order anything seeing as we sold out of most items earlier. I'm smiling as I put the last utensil away. Not a bad problem to have for a Thursday night. I mentally pat myself on the back. It still sneaks up on me, knowing that so many people have my back and believe in me. My heart warms.

When I don't hear the bell again, signaling someone's exit, I decide I had better go take care of this so we can close up and I can let Anna go home. It's only after I step through the back swinging door into the front of the shop that I see the reason she hasn't let our customer know we're closed.

Barrett Holloway, all 6'4", tattooed muscle, greek god of him, is leaning against the counter, chatting politely with a very flushed and flustered Anna. He's maybe the last person I expected to be here. I knew it was a possibility that he would be back in town, having heard about his knee injury. I just didn't think it would be so soon. I haven't really spoken to him in four years. In fact, I've tried to avoid any one-on-one interaction with him at all costs since I went to one of his hockey games to confess how much I missed him and wanted to be with him. Instead of giving the 'it's always been you' speech and him taking me in his arms and sealing our love with a kiss, I found out he had a girlfriend.

Yes, that was mortifying, and I try not to think about it too often. I say try because when I lay down in bed at night and wade through the sea of embarrassing memories (past, present, and future) that particularly painful memory never fails to float to the surface. It's because of those dark anxiety ridden moments, that I have thought about how a conversation between us would go after all this time. There are actually multiple variations of how I have pictured this in my head.

So, why in my moment of need couldn't any of those one sided conversations make their way to the forefront of my brain? If I had to guess the reason, it would be that in all of my delusional scenarios, my poor brain did an abysmal job at remembering him correctly. God, he's breathtaking.

Then he turns his full sparkling gaze on me, I forget to catch the swinging door–

"*Shit!*" I hear his deep voice in sync with my own.

Well, this was definitely not one of the scenarios I was prepared for.

RHETT

I swipe the steam from the mirror over the sink in the hotel bathroom. I take a good look at myself then blow out a breath. I look awful. My eyes are bloodshot and I have dark circles under them. The drive from Seattle to Silverthorne was brutal. Nineteen hours, 1300 miles in a truck by yourself gives you plenty of time to think about all the choices you've made and second guess them, but standing in that arena earlier today with my new team solidified that I was in the right place. I've thought about what leaving behind my life in the city will be like and how excited I am to be back in Colorado. To be back in my hometown with my family and friends is what I need in my life right now.

I'm almost out of the hotel before I completely know what I'm doing. I told myself that I just needed to go for a walk before bed but if I'm being honest, there's only one place I'll be walking to. I know she opened her own bakery a few months back. Colt mentioned it in passing when he called to ask about my injury. I have tried not to think about her over the years but the way we ended never sat right with me.

My mom calls as I'm pulling on my jacket. It may be August but when the sun goes down you'll be sorry you don't have an extra layer handy.

"Hey, mom."

"You got in today didn't you?" She asks without so much as a 'hey'.

"I did. Just this morning. I took a nap after I met with the team and had a shower. Sorry I forgot to call."

"Oh, that's fine. Your sister called me to let me know you checked in." Then why did she ask? "I'm still not sure why you're staying there when you know we have plenty of rooms here at the ranch."

"Yeah mom, I know I'm welcome to stay with you and dad until I can move into the house, but I'm fine staying at the hotel for now." I've already bought a house and had the inspection. I'm only waiting to sign the papers next week.

"Okay, well it's an open invite, dear." I can't help the way my lips tip upward, knowing this won't be the last time she offers.

"Thank you, mom. I'll keep it in mind. I'll see you tomorrow for lunch."

"See you tomorrow, Rhett." She sighs. "I can't wait to have all my kids together again, it's been too long." I know she's thrilled to have us all in town again. She's been on Knox and Alder lately about settling down and needing more grandkids to spoil...I know it will be my turn next.

"Looking forward to it, mom. Love you."

"Love you, son."

I slip my phone in my pocket, look down the empty sidewalk and head in the direction I've been drawn to since I arrived in town this afternoon.

When I accepted the coaching job for the High School, I knew it was the right decision. I like to think I'm a simple man. There are only a few things I want in life and being back in Silverthorne for good is one of them. After being away for the last eight years on and off, traveling with my team, the Seattle Hornets, I've only been able to visit for certain holidays and important milestones. I've tried to be there for as much as I can, but an NHL players schedule is pretty packed.

I take in the sleepy mountain town. Silverthorne is exactly the same. The mountains are comforting as ever and with fall on its way and hockey season around the corner I'm feeling at peace with being here. I love this place and always have. Not only does this place have one of the best views but it also has some of the best people.

Now I get to be close to my family. I was the only one left of the four of us that didn't live in town. I'm excited to see more of my siblings. My older brothers, my perfect little niece, my baby sister, and of course my parents. It would be near to impossible to find better people than Tom and Mary Holloway. My best friend since high school is here, running his own rafting business. Living here will mean spending my weekends fishing, hiking, and rafting again. Outdoor sports played a huge role in my upbringing and my love for them has only grown. Camping trips are few and far between when you're traveling all over the country two or three times a week, seven months out of the year. Then there's practices and training camps. Don't get me wrong, I loved every minute of it. The adrenaline of being out on the ice, the high that comes from a big win, it's like nothing else...but I'm ready to slow down a bit and even if I wasn't, my sore knee is.

I round the corner and see my destination still has the lights on. That's a good sign. I make my way inside and see a young girl behind the counter looking down at her phone.

"Hey there, you all still open?" I do my best to announce myself because I'm not sure if the bell chime was enough. She briefly looks up, registers my presence, snaps her head in my direction, then stuffs her phone into the front pocket of her apron. She puts on a bashful smile.

"Um, hi," she squeaks out. "I'll have to check with Winnie. She's the owner." Just then I hear a shout from the back telling the girl, Anna, that they're supposed to be closed. She blushes so I fill the silence.

"Sounds like I'm out of luck tonight, I'll just have to come back in the morning I suppose." I say with a wink. Anna blushes further.

"Oh, yeah...that's a good idea. We um, we're open from 5am till noon on Saturdays..." She trails off and I give her another smile.

"I'll come by tomorrow then."

"That's probably a good idea if you want a cinnamon roll. They sell out fast in the mornings."

"I'll make sure I'm here at open then." I wink and she giggles. I'm getting ready to turn around and regretfully make my way back to the hotel when I hear footsteps heading our way. I look up in time to see honey eyes that I've on more-than-one occasion wanted to melt into. Yeah, playing in the NHL was a dream come true but another dream of mine, the one I barely even admit to myself, she just got smacked in the face with a swinging door.

"Shit!" we say in unison. I make my way around the counter and over to her side. Winslow Parker is holding the right side of her face and muttering curses under her breath. *Damn.* She's more beautiful than the last time I saw her. Her dark unruly hair is haphazardly trapped on top of her head with a pencil sticking through and she's wearing a black apron, smattered with flour, with her Thistle and Sage logo on the front.

"Jeezes, Winnie. Are you alright?" She smiles or at least attempts to. It's a cross between a smile and a grimace.

"Why would you think I wasn't?" She says breezily, but I can tell it's painful. A smile tugs at my lips. I have really missed her. "Oh this?" She uses her free hand to gesture to the one covering her face. "This is nothing. Happens all the time and this isn't even the worst." She does this. Always has. Minimizes pain. Feelings...especially her own.

"Okay, tough guy, let me see." I put my hands on her narrow shoulders and direct her over to one of the tables. I slide two chairs together and nudge her to sit down on one while I sit on the other. My left hand goes to her elbow and the other gently tries to tip her head up so I can get a good look at the side of her face that was just hit. She waves a hand in the air as she tries to brush off the incident and the pain she is probably in.

"I'm fine, really. As I'm sure you know, it's not the first time I've run into a door and I'm sure it won't be the last." I'm not buying it. They had to have heard the impact of the hit outside.

"Come on Winnie, just let me take a look." She relents and lets me gently pull her hand away from her heart shaped face. I look at her high cheekbone, it's red and already a little swollen. Her full bottom lip looks slightly more full, but it's not split.

RHETT   17

"How bad is it? Am I gonna make it?" She asks with just the slightest bit of snark. I chuckle.

"Hey Anna?" I look at the girl behind the counter. "Do you think you could find an ice pack and a towel for Winnie?" She's already walking through the offending door when she calls back to me.

"On it!"

When I look back and meet Winnie's topaz gaze, I'm momentarily stunned.

Winslow Parker with a dazed expression from across the bakery was stunning, but having her close, touching her injured, splotchy, but still beautiful face, she's *devastating*. I shake my head to clear it of thoughts that I need to get a handle on.

"Hi, Rhett." Her smirk has softened to one of her sweet smiles and I don't know if I've felt this warm since the last time I was this close to her.

She does that, too. Emits warmth.

"Hi, Winnie." I'm holding her cheek against my palm when Anna comes back, holding up a piping bag of ice and a hand towel.

"Will this work? It's all I could find back there." She takes in my hand resting gently against Winnie's face and a sugges-tive smile curves her lips. "If you don't need me for anything else I can head out." She raises her eyebrows at Winnie and gives her a pointed look.

"That's fine, Anna. Go ahead and get home. I'll see you tomorrow."

"I'm really sorry you got hurt again tonight." Anna remarks and Winnie winces.

"*Again?*" I question and I know the look on my face shows

I'm worried. She shoots an annoyed expression at Anna, and I stifle a laugh. She keeps her tone light when she replies.

"Don't worry about me. I'll see you in the morning."

"Sure, Winnie." She sighs before grabbing her bag from behind the counter. "I'm gonna have to keep a closer eye on you, ya know? We've only been open for a few months and I swear you've gotten hurt like once a week. You burned your hand on the oven, tripped while you were carrying in the bags of sugar, the day you hit the back of your head on the counter standing up and now this?" Winnie grits her teeth and looks at the ceiling, collecting herself.

"Anna, I'll be fine. Thanks for all your help tonight."

"No problem. Sorry your date had to be canceled." *Date?* "See you in the morning." She turns her attention to me next as she walks for the door. "It was really nice to meet you um..."

"Rhett." I supply.

"Rhett...um yeah, nice to meet you." As she talks she looks back to Winnie. "Please make sure Winslow doesn't trip or slip or hurt herself any more tonight, please." She smiles sweetly and winks before continuing her way out. I give her my most charming smile.

"I'll see what I can do. Bye, Anna." I glance at Winnie to find her blushing but with a hard set to her jaw.

Anna slips through the door, and I go to lock it behind her, flipping the *Open* sign to *Closed*. I look back at Winnie and take in her embarrassed expression. She's beautiful and I can't help but tease her.

"So, it sounds like this may be a regular occurrence here." She rolls her eyes at me.

"It's not a secret that I'm not the most...graceful." She begrudgingly says the last word.

"You?! Not graceful? This is news to me." I can't help the laugh that escapes me. Over the many years I've known Winnie, I have witnessed countless incidents that involved only her and a flat surface. My sarcasm doesn't even warrant a laugh from her, she just stares at me, but before I can place the expression she lets out a sigh.

"I have actually been hiking more recently and I haven't fallen off any cliffs yet." She laughs but I can't stop my wince because the idea of Winnie out on a trail alone really does concern me.

"You really shouldn't be out there alone, Winnie." She rolls her eyes, dismissing my concern for her.

"Who said I was alone?" That's right. Anna mentioned a *date*. She may have a boyfriend. While I'm contemplating asking if that's the case, she continues.

"You know this..." She points to her ice covered face... "... wouldn't have happened if *someone* hadn't flustered my employee into forgetting we were closed."

I feign outrage.

"*Me?* Surely you don't really think your lack of spatial awareness is my fault?" She gives me an absolutely knowing look.

"What is that look for?" She snorts.

"Just you being your charming self. Making that poor girl blush from head to toe. I guess I should be used to it by now."

"You think I'm charming?" I wiggle my eyebrows and my question elicits another eye roll, but she lets out a laugh.

"Barrett Holloway, it's really not like you to act oblivious to your allure. In all the years I've known you and all the conversations between you and Colt that I've been privy to, it's usually a point of pride for you." I grin. I can't help it. I know that I'm attractive, there have been plenty of women over the years who've told me I am. Including her. I've never been at a loss for a woman's company. I may not be oblivious to how women react to me, but I really like hearing Winnie say it.

"Well, Ms. Parker. I won't apologize for being raised right and knowing how to treat a lady." That gets me a bigger laugh.

"Is that what you're calling it then? 'Treating a lady right?' I may know some of your heeaartbroken..." she drags the word out for effect... "girls from high school and even a few women here in town that might argue that point." Okay, if that's how she wants to play this.

"What about you?" I ask and her face changes as she registers my question. She's putting up her walls.

"What about me?" Her tone lets me know I've pressed a button.

"Would you argue the point?" She looks startled by my question and even I'm a little caught off guard by the shift in intensity. She swallows.

"That was a long time ago, Rhett." She says it so quietly I'm not sure I've heard her correctly. "So, how long are you in town for this time?" Her question throws me, not only because she hasn't answered my question, but I thought she would have known. She talks to my mother most days, I know this because I make it a point to ask how she is when I talk to my mother. They've been thick as thieves since she and Colt moved to town to live with their uncle. Winnie needed someone in her life to help her get through the death of her parents and mom threw herself into the role, falling in love with Winnie like most people in this town.

"For quite awhile. Permanently, actually." Her eyes go wide.

"P...permanently?" she asks. She's flustered and I find it adorable.

"Yeah, I would have thought mom would have let you know. Or Colt. I talked to him about this just last week. I bought a house and will be taking over as the High School hockey coach in the fall." She takes in my words for a beat then softly responds.

"I was sorry to hear about your knee. So, you're really done playing hockey?" I let out a breath. No one's asked me this question that really cares about the answer.

"I don't know if I'll ever be done playing hockey, but I'm done playing professionally."

"...and are you okay with that?" She nudges her leg against mine. A small touch but I heat at the contact. I clear my throat.

"Not sure I have much of a choice, but I am happy to be back in town and I'm excited for the opportunity to coach these boys."

"Wow, Rhett. That's really exciting." I can't stop the smirk that appears at her monotone reply.

"Yeah, you sound really excited, Winnie." I deadpan then let out a chuckle. "Will it be so awful to have me around?" Something flashes across her face, too quickly for me to name and she looks me in the eyes.

"Of course it won't be. I really am happy you'll be closer to your family. I know they all miss you so much." She smiles and it's genuine. Then she looks up and I can sense a shift in her as she stands. "Well. I need to finish up closing so I can get home. Another early morning here tomorrow. Thanks for checking me out, Rhett..." I smirk and her neck and uninjured cheek tinge pink and she rushes to rephrase. "...er for looking at my face....for making sure I'm okay," she stammers. It's so cute I can't help my grin. "Thanks for stopping by. I guess I'll be seeing you around town." She practically pushes me toward the door.

"No problem. I'm glad you're okay, but you should keep some ice on your cheek tonight to help with the swelling."

"Sure, sure. I'll do that. Bye, Rhett."

"See you in the morning, Winnie." She looks confused.

"In the morning?" My cheeks hurt from trying to hide my smile.

"Yeah, I hear I'll have to get here early in the morning if I want any of your baked goods."

"Right, yes. Well...I'll see you then...maybe. I'm usually working in the back but Anna will be out front taking orders and she'll make sure you get something good." She's rambling now and I'm not used to seeing her this worked up or what to make of it.

"Alright then, goodnight."

"Night, Rhett." I feel a light shove at my hip and hear the door shut and lock shut behind me. Not exactly how I had hoped she would receive the news of my being back in town for good. How did I want her to react? Did I want her to be excited because *she* wanted me back in town? Yeah, I'm not sure that's warranted...but the way she reacted just then?

That was not on my list of possibilities.

RHETT

I start the walk back to my family's hotel after practically being shoved out of Winnie's bakery. It's quiet, just the sound of my footfalls and thoughts of our conversation fill my ears. The way she looked at me gave me the impression that she still might think about me the way I have her over the years. Maybe I mis-read her being polite for fondness at seeing me this evening. She got cagey on me when I told her I would be staying in town.

I'm almost to my room and heading straight to bed so I can get up early tomorrow morning to see Winnie—*no, stop Rhett*—to visit the bakery to show my support for her new business. My mom and all my siblings have been talking nonstop the last few months about all the delicious things that come out of Winnie's kitchen. I love the pride in mom's voice when she talks about her. I could do without the photo Alder sent me with his arms wrapped around Winnie, kissing her cheek.

As I'm reaching for my keycard, I feel my phone vibrate in my jacket pocket. When I pull it out, I'm greeted with the sight of me and my best friend. We're decked out in snowboarding gear and huge smiles, I think we were maybe 17. I tap the screen and answer.

"Hey, Colt. What's up?"

"When did you get in, man?"

"Just this morning. I haven't had much time to do anything other than settle in at the hotel." I don't tell him about visiting Winnie at her bakery and I'm not sure why because there's no reason I shouldn't visit her and check out her new business.

"Well, why don't you come out to AJ's and have a drink? You're only just across the way."

"I don't know man, I'm pretty beat and have to be up early in the morning." *To see your sister who at this point in time seems to not want to see me.*

"Aw, come on, it's been forever since we've been in the same town! I need my wingman back!" Well now I really had no desire to go, but if I was being honest with myself, I was too keyed up from my interaction with Winnie to fall asleep any time soon anyway.

"Okay, I'll be there in five, one drink."

Colt gives me a "Hell Yeah!" and hangs up before I can respond. I smile at his enthusiasm. He's always been charismatic. When he and Winnie moved here we became fast friends. If Colt's jumping off a cliff, I'm already in the water having jumped right before. I've never broached the subject of Winnie with him and when I wanted to back then, she didn't want me to. Saying it didn't matter if we were only for the summer anyway. I scrub a hand down my face, trying to clear thoughts of that summer and Winnie from my mind before I'm sitting next to her brother for the next hour.

I turn back down the hall and make my way across the street.

Angry James, AJ's, isn't the only bar in town, but it may as well be as far as locals are concerned. As soon as I walk through the front door I'm hit with memories. Mostly good, only a few bad.

"Rhett!" I hear my name and see Colt's arm waving around in the air to signal me. The motion isn't necessary because even though it's always busy in here, it's only about 600 square feet. I give him a wave to let him know I've seen him and then make my way to the bar to order my one and only beer of the night. I grin when I spot the owner, Buck, behind the counter.

"Barrett Holloway, is it true I'll be seeing you more around here?"

"Hey Buck, yes it's true. You'll have to put up with my mug regularly. I'll be taking over Coach Reynolds' position at the high school."

"Well I'll be. I know your mom and dad are sure gonna be happy to have you around more. A few ladies in town may be as well." There's a twinkle in his eyes that seems to always be present. Buck's been a fixture in our community for as far back as I can remember. He has a booth at every festival this town puts on month after month and donates to local food pantry. He organizes and works the annual toy drive in December, along with playing Santa. He's also Colt and Winnie's uncle.

"What can I get ya, son?"

"Can I get whatever IPA's on tap tonight?"

"You got it." I glance around the room to see if I recognize more faces in here. Colt's sitting at a table closer to the corner and it looks like he's got a couple of women I don't recognize sitting across from him. I'm really not wanting to chat up anyone for him tonight but here we are. Buck sets my beer on the bartop and I nod.

"Thanks, Buck." He nods back and moves on to the couple at the end of the counter. I take a sip, then amble over to Colt's table. He's tapping on his phone, but looks up when I reach the table.

"Hey, man!" I set my beer down just in time for Colt to slam into me and lock me in a bear hug. I return the hug and pat his back a few times.

"Hey Colt, how have you been?"

"Good, good. Business has really taken off the last couple of years, so I can't complain."

Colt started his own white water rafting business about five years ago. He takes groups to raft all over the state.

"That's great. Think you'll have time to get out on the river with me in the next couple weeks? I've been itching to get back in a boat."

"If we end up with a good rain like we did last season, absolutely! You know I'll make time for you." He turns back to the table then and introduces me. "Rhett, this is Georgia and Lucy, they're passing through on their cross country roadtrip and looking to white water raft while they're here. Ladies, this is Rhett Holloway." Both their mouths drop open.

"Nice to meet you, ladies." They both hold their hands up and say 'hi'.

"Rhett Holloway as in, Rhett Holloway, the Seattle Hornets Right Winger? What are you doing here?" The one with dark hair, Lucy asks.

"Actually, this is my hometown. I blew my knee out at the

end of last season and decided to trade my pads for a whistle.
I'll be coaching here in town at the high school this fall."

"Oh, that sucks. I'm so sorry to hear that," she says,
sounding genuine. I smile. I see Colt check his phone out of the
corner of my eye and whisper something to the blonde.

"It may have happened a little differently than I expected
but it's always been the plan to be back here in Silverthorne."

"Are you gonna miss living in Seattle?" The other one,
Georgia, asks.

"A bit, It'll be an adjustment going from the city scene to
small town living, but to be honest I'm not one for big cities."
She smiles brightly.

"I love Seattle!" Lucy interjects, smiling widely. "I've been
able to visit quite a few times. I love going to the market and
taking the ferry! My cousin lives out on Bainbridge Island." I
smile back.

"It was a change of pace for sure. The city is a little too
busy for me but I did enjoy the ferry, and getting to hike in
Olympic when I actually had some free time, Overall I did
enjoy my time there."

As I'm speaking she leans in and puts her hand on my
forearm that's folded on the table next to my beer. I'm trying to
think of a way to pull my arm back without it being too
awkward.

I notice Colt check his phone again, smile and glance at the
door. I follow his line of sight and there standing in the
doorway of AJ's is Winnie. She see's Colt, waves and smiles
and starts toward our table. Her eyes meet mine and her smile
dims a little, then she looks down to see Lucy's hand resting on
my arm and it disappears entirely. Great.

WINNIE

"Win!" I hear my brother yell my name as I keep walking towards his table but I'm staring a hole in Rhett's forearm. A tattooed, more attractive than it should be, forearm, where a hand is attached to a gorgeous brunette I've never seen before, is still resting. Seriously. He's been in town less than a day and already has a woman on his arm. Literally. This does not bode well for my sanity. *Get a grip, Winslow. You're an adult, not some lovestruck teenager with a crush anymore.* I scold myself and tear my eyes away and look up at Colt just as he reaches me for a hug.

"Hey, Colt. I've got your keys...again." I say as sweetly as I can. "You've got to start checking your pockets. This is the second time this month." He laughs and when he does it's hard to stay annoyed at him. I love my brother. He has been my rock since I was thirteen and had to move across the country to a town we had only been to once, to live with an uncle we had only met twice. Thankfully, that uncle was Uncle Buck, who turned out to be exactly who we needed after we lost our parents and a truly amazing man.

"Yeah, Win, I know. I'll try to keep better track of my truck keys." He kisses the top of my head. "Thanks for bringing the spare set to me." I can tell when he gets a good look at me because his eyes widen. "What happened to your face??" I wince. The ice I've had on it the last 20 minutes has helped with the swelling but it's still red and will probably bruise.

"I was just closing up over at the bakery and the swinging door was talking back." I glance back to the table and see that Rhett has leaned back in his chair, forearms now folded across his chest. The brunette's hand is now holding her drink. I smile politely at her and Colt sighs before he starts introductions.

"Please be more careful with yourself, Win. I hate it when you get hurt like this." I try for a reassuring smile even though he's annoying me. He turns his attention back to the table.

"Ladies, this is my sister, Winnie. Win, this is Lucy and Georgia." Lucy, the gorgeous brunette...*with wandering hands*...gives me a smile. It's a pretty smile and kind, which annoys me further.

"Hey there, nice to meet you! So, do you raft, too?" she asks animatedly. Neither Colt or Rhett can stop their laughter. I cast a withering look at them both, then look back at a waiting Lucy.

"Actually..." I tuck some hair that's escaped my pencil bun behind my ear and shift on my feet. "...white water isn't really my thing."

"That's an understatement." Rhett chimes in. "The last time you were on a raft you lost your paddle, fell out twice, and screamed bloody murder any time we hit some waves." He and Colt are wheezing now and Georgia and Lucy have joined them. My cheeks are absolutely scorching with the knowledge he remembers that awful day. I had only gone to spend time with *him* and it was an experience that I could live out the rest of my days happily without repeating.

"Right, well, it was nice to meet you both." I nod at both the girls, wishing the ground would swallow me but my next best move is to get out of here before anyone decides to reveal the handful of times I tried snowboarding. The girls both nod back while still chuckling a little. I look at my brother. "Colt, just bring those keys by the bakery tomorrow so I have them for the next time you try to do two things at once." I bite out from behind a fake smile.

"Oh come on Win, don't run off. I'm sorry." He's still smiling but sobered a bit. "Outdoor sports just aren't your thing. Baking though..." He winks to the table. "...no one even comes close." I give him a tight smile. Like I said, it's hard to stay upset with Colt.

"I've got to get up early to open the bakery anyway, but I'll see you later." I look at the table again, toward *him*. "Rhett, good to see you again." He drops his head as he speaks, not looking up. "Yep, good to see you Winslow." *Winslow...?* I don't think he's called me that since...well I'm not sure when he stopped calling me Winslow and started calling me Winnie, but hearing him say my full name sounds odd.

I give a little wave and head toward the door, but before I make it that far I spot my uncle wiping down the bar and decide I better check in. It's been a couple days since I've seen him and I've missed him.

"Hey Uncle Buck!" I call out before I knock my knuckles against the counter. He gives me one of his big smiles, eyes twinkling like always as he flips the little latch on the bartop to come around.

"Hey, sweetheart! What are you doing out this late?" I give him a look and throw an amused glance at my brother. "Again?" He whistles. "That boy would forget his ass if it wasn't attached to the rest of him." I let out a laugh and I sag a little into his embrace as he reaches me for a hug. I didn't realize how tired I was or how tense.

"How's business?" he asks, even though he's been to my bakery every day since I opened.

"It's good, real good actually. I can't believe how busy we've been. I was even asked to set up a booth at the End Of Summer Festival." His smile gets bigger.

"I don't know why you're so surprised young lady. You're so talented when it comes to food, just like your mom. And you know this community adores you." My eyes mist and I blame it on an emotional rollercoaster of a night I've had and exhaustion.

"Yeah, well it helps that I've got you in my corner." I need to get out of here and get into bed before I start crying. The day has finally caught up with me and though I'm not really that sad to be parting ways with Sam, it could've ended better. So I give Uncle Buck one last squeeze and kiss his cheek. "I'll see you tomorrow. Maybe I can stop in for a bit after closing up."

"Sounds good, sweetheart, but don't worry if you can't. I know you'll be busy with getting things ready for Saturday. I'm really proud of you, you know?" He clears his throat. "Your parents would be, too." That does it. My throat goes tight and I can feel a couple tears escape my now blurry eyes. I swipe them away quickly and reinforce the dam.

"Alright, enough of that." I'm barely keeping it together as is. "I love you, Buck."

"Love you too, kiddo." He winks and I finally head toward the door and home, finally. I decide to torture myself and sneak one more peak at Rhett, but when I do he's already looking at me with a thoughtful expression pulling his eyebrows together. He's looked at me like this before and it takes me back to a time when he wanted to know everything in my head, but I wouldn't let him in.

I trip over the entry rug, just enough to make me stumble and inwardly cringe. I can feel my cheeks heat as I catch myself. I am a walking disaster tonight. I do not look back at him again as I walk through the door, not only because I don't want to see his reaction, but also because I should really be watching where I'm going.

The cool night air calms me a little and helps with my flaming face. I turn in the direction of my house and make the small trek there. One of the many things I love about living in Silverthorne is that I can walk or bike anywhere...mostly walk since that small biking incident. I wince remembering Janet Tilley, the local florist, letting out a gasp, a look of horror on her face as I hit the curb in front of her shop, landing on the sidewalk. I walked away with just a skinned elbow and knee. Definitely could have been worse with my track record, still embarrassing though.

I really have been trying to get out in nature more. I love exploring the state parks and swimming in the rivers. I can't help it that I wasn't blessed with a normal amount of coordination. I let out a breath and turn the last corner to my house. I live right next to the old historic district, the house next door is one of my favorites. Just a couple blocks over from the bakery, which is perfect. I've been renovating it while living there.

I love it.

It's small, just a two bedroom, one bath cottage really, but perfect for me. I walk next to the black metal fence till I get to my gate. I swing it open and make my way down the small walkway. I just got all the brick pavers put in last month and I smile every time I look out at them. A light from inside glows and lights my path as I climb the concrete steps, seeing my porch swing on the other side. I grab my keys to unlock my front door and enter my own little safe haven.

I step inside and flip the deadbolt into place, slip off my shoes, and toss my jacket on the chair. I'm too tired to do much of anything and my bed is calling my name, but the slight sting still pulsing on the right side of my face has me reaching for an ice pack and towel out of the kitchen on the way to my bedroom. I quickly change into my pajamas, because I always change into pajamas, and crawl into my cozy bed, ice pack firmly pressed to my cheek. 4 AM will be here in less than seven hours and I need sleep if I'm going to have to face Rhett again tomorrow.

Seeing him twice in one day, after having found my boyfriend sleeping with another woman...what a day.

WINNIE

I dream of emerald eyes and full lips smiling at me before coming close to mine. Hands that steadied me at the bakery are now exploring other parts of my body, skimming my thighs and making their way up, *"Do you like that, Winnie?"* Oh, god. His voice is husky in my ear and he inches closer, so close to the place I need it most, almost there...*beep, beep, beep, beep!*

"No!" I shout into the damp towel stuck to my face. I barely feel like I've slept at all when my alarm goes off. I groan. Surely it's not morning yet. I crack one eye open, reaching for my phone to shut it up. Ah, definitely morning. It looks like I've slept through my alarm for the past 15 minutes. Great.

I know it was only a dream but that was as close as I've been to getting any in...awhile. Let's just say Sam was extremely passionate...about his peach orchard and literally nothing else. It's not like we never had sex. It's just that the three or four times we did over the last six months seemed to progressively get worse. I cringe at the mental image of the last time we were intimate. I couldn't even convincingly fake it.

I blow out a breath and my lips flutter with the action. Maybe Mare is right. *I can never admit to her.* Before I started dating Sam she had been on me about getting on dating apps again. Saying that if I wanted casual then that would be the way to do it. The thing is I don't think casual *is* what I want. I just can't seem to get myself to commit when the time comes. I'm definitely an all or nothing girl. I've had a few one night stands but for the most part I'm monogamous. I'm a relationship girl, even if the relationship doesn't last longer than a month. The way I feel right now though, extremely hot and bothered, her suggestion to go out and maybe...possibly...have a casual sexual experience without the threat of a relationship, is tempting.

I finally toss my covers back and swing my legs over the side of the bed. If I don't get ready now I will for sure be late getting the pastries out this morning. I slide into my slippers and go to my closet. I usually try to gather my clothes for the morning, the night before, but last night...last night was a shit show. I grab a pair of jeans and a simple white baby tee. This will have to do. I don't have time to second guess my outfit today or take a shower. I sniff my armpits, not terrible but I will be applying deodorant.

I splash some cold water on my face to wake up, the swelling is gone. Mostly. It's just a bit red. I apply my moisturizer and sunscreen, chapstick, and mascara. I pull my thick tangled hair back to pile it up into a claw clip I realize I left on my nightstand last night. I head back into my bedroom to retrieve the clip and get changed. I grab my phone from the nightstand and beeline for the door.

One of the amazing things about having my own bakery is I can get coffee and breakfast at work. I pick up my jacket from the chair I tossed it on last night, slip my sneakers on, swing my bag over my shoulder and walk out into the still dark morning. I stop for just a second on my front porch and inhale deeply. It's nice out this morning with a slight breeze but that's another great thing about living in Silverthorne. Cooler in the mornings, that is until the sun's heat tries to roast you like a rotisserie chicken.

I love this time of day. It's so quiet and peaceful on the street as I go to work to do what I love to do, in a place I love doing it. It reminds me to take a minute to be grateful. I may have had a rough couple years after the accident, I still have days where my anxiety fights for control, but I realize I have so much in my life to be thankful for.

I make it to the bakery just before 3:30. I'm here even earlier than normal today to make items for the festival tomorrow. I don't need to start my breads and pastries until 4, so I take a second to admire my sign. Thistle and Sage has been my labor of love. My dream that with hard work and support has become my reality. I beam looking up at the storefront then move to go inside. Right before I head in, I turn my head to look at the Holloway Hotel.

It's just a block over and soon I'll be seeing Rhett coming and going regularly. It's not exactly an *unwelcome* thought, but I would be lying if selfishly I didn't think it would make things a little harder for me. When he was away at school it was just the summers I had to get through. Actually, I looked forward to him coming home for the summers until *that summer*. He had just been drafted into the NHL and the whole town was buzzing with that news. Colt was just getting his rafting business started and I was in my second year of pastry school.

I'd had a crush on Rhett Holloway starting from the day I turned sixteen. He gave me a pink sprinkle doughnut and a kiss on my cheek and that was all it took. Yes, his brothers both gave me a treat and a kiss on my cheek, too. It wasn't the same to me though. The moment Rhett's lips made contact with my bright red face, I was done for.

I sometimes try to convince myself it was simply because of the exposure. I spent almost every afternoon at his house with Mary. She had made an effort the first day I moved to town and there was just something about her that let me know she was going to be important to me. If I wasn't at his house hanging out with his mom or his sister Florence, he was at mine with Colt. A couple years older than me and gorgeous. I'm only one of many many girls who fell under his spell—one he didn't even know he was casting.

Lord, I followed them around like a lost puppy until I turned seventeen and decided to try and turn his head. I let out a half laugh at how ridiculous I was. I inwardly cringe at how obvious I was. To everyone but him at least. I was infatuated. A teenage girl, possessed.

On my 17th birthday I wore the smallest bikini I could find. It was bright orange with hot pink ties. We went down to the river for a cookout and swimming. He wouldn't even look at me most of the day besides to say a quick *"Happy Birthday"* that sounded like Mary had forced him to give me. A few other boys in my grade took notice, so I knew I didn't look horrible, but the one person I wanted to notice couldn't be bothered. I let out a sad sigh because that was when I made the choice to stop my romanticizing and fantasies.

Barrett Halloway was out of my league and now I had confirmation. I still saw him almost everyday after that, until he went to college that fall and then it was only for those few warm months every year and the occasional holiday visit. We were still friendly and I was still a tagalong little sister. Colt and I have always been close. It's never been out of place to see me with them. While they did their snowboarding, I read books inside at the ski lodge. I sunbathed on the bank of the river where they were paddling or rafting.

It wasn't until *that summer* I realized Rhett may see me more than just Colt's little sister. He was home for two months before moving to a new city and starting his career as a professional hockey player. We went camping out by the lake by his family's property a couple nights after he got back. It was supposed to just be a few of us but of course Colt had invited a few girls I didn't know and they had invited other people I didn't know.

I don't always do well with large groups, especially not ones where I don't know more than half the people. That's all Colt. He's happy go lucky, spontaneous and fun. I'm...not. I'm sharper, calculated. I like to know the plan and sometimes when I don't know the plan I get irritable. I pick a fight and throw the first punch. I can't always pull it back either.

That night after having made so much small talk you could fill the Grand Canyon I decided to remove myself from the equation. Some of the guys here were cute. A couple of them seemed sweet and interested in hearing about pastry school, but I could feel my ears getting hot. The longer I spent making sure I was smiling or nodding at the right times was getting to me and I was getting mean.

I walked away from the bonfire and the noise created by all

the drunk people. I just needed some space and a little quiet. I sat on a big rock at the edge of the lake, slipped my shoes off and let my feet dangle below just grazing the cold water below. I felt calmer already. That was until I heard a twig snap and I whipped my head around to see a tall form walking towards me. I was ready to scream until I heard that deep voice.

"Hey, honeybee."

I push through the front door of my bakery as I push the past from my mind. It has never served me well to dwell on it, and believe I've done that a lot. I'm standing in my beautiful kitchen when I flip on the lights and the ovens. I get to work making baked goods for the people that would be filing inside in about an hour. I focus on what my hands are doing. I like baking because it combines mental work with a physical task. I have to measure everything exactly right and knead and roll and add things at the right time or it won't turn out. Forty-five minutes of peace later I hear Anna get in.

"Winnie! I'm out front. I'm gonna start putting the chairs down!" she yells as the bell chimes.

"Thanks, Anna!" I yell back. My pastries and breakfast breads are just about done. We open in 10 minutes. I start loading trays up to put in the font case.

"How are you this morning, Anna?"

"I'm good besides it being entirely too early on a Saturday." She says through a yawn. "How's the face?" I laugh.

"My face is fine, thanks. You know, when you applied for this job I did specify that it would involve early morning Saturdays."

"You did, I just didn't realize how early it would feel until I actually had to do it. I'm good though...is there any coffee?" She smiles sweetly and I roll my eyes.

"Yes, go ahead and get a cup before customers start coming in." She grins and races into the back while I finish filling the glass cases. She's back five minutes later with a little more pep. "Alright, you ready for a busy Saturday?" I ask.

"Absolutely." She genuinely sounds excited and I beam. "I'll get the door and sign!"

I move to the swinging door that caused a commotion last night and a bruise to be forming on my face today and laugh at myself. How ridiculous must I have seemed to Rhett last night? Oh, well. No need dwelling on it now. Hopefully I won't have to see him today...or for a few days. The first *Ding!* sounds just as I'm through the door. Wow it's only just now 5, someone's up early this morning.

"Good morning, Anna." *That voice.*

Husky from the early morning it sounds even more like the one I woke to...er from...this morning. I'm blushing hard, remembering what the body attached to that voice was about to do to me in my dream. I stop that thought in its tracks. I haven't blushed this much since I was in high school and he's only been here a day. *Get a grip, Winnie.* I start stacking metal bowls and try to focus on anything other than my dream. He doesn't think of me like that anymore and I need to accept that. I pull out my phone and send a text to Mare, telling her I'll go out next weekend for my birthday.

RHETT

I'm barely moving as I walk on the sidewalk to Winnie's bakery. I probably don't need to be there right at open but I told her I would be. I only stayed at the bar with Colt last night until I finished my beer. And it wasn't a lie when I told him I was running on fumes. My day caught up to me like a ton of bricks. I said goodnight to Georgia and Lucy, much to Lucy's dismay and passed out in my hotel room. Hard.

Town is quiet and peaceful this morning. I actually like this time of day just not when I've not driven across the country the day before. This is my favorite time to go for a run. Well, starting about four months ago when I was cleared for exercise, it's more of a jog. I'm more limited physically than I even have been. Sure, I'll still be on the ice with my team and I'll be mountain biking on the weekends, but now I'll be paying for it in ice baths and elevation.

I step into Thistle and Sage and am greeted by the smell of cinnamon and fresh bread and Anna.

"Good morning! You're up early." Anna is smiling at me from her spot behind the counter.

"I am, I heard if I wanted to get the good stuff, I had to be here early."

"That is absolutely true. Winslow has just got the front fully stocked, what can I get for you?"

"Well let's see, my mom says the cinnamon rolls are the best, so can I get one of those and also a cup of coffee?"

"Coming right up!" She busies herself with getting my pastry and coffee and I take the time to look around the little shop, wondering if I'm going to get the chance to see Winnie this morning. I made sure to be the first one here before they have their rush, hoping to say hello. "Did you want to eat this here or do you want me to put it in a box to go?"

"I'll eat it here, thanks Anna."

"Yep. Here ya go. Let me know if you need anything else."

"Uh...Is Winnie busy this morning?" She smirks.

"Winnie is always busy, but I can check to see if she has a minute if you want." I give her a wink.

"I'd appreciate that." She only blushes a little at that. I sit down at a table in the corner and dig into this amazing smelling cinnamon roll while I wait. There's a clatter in the back, then I hear Winnie curse, I can't help but chuckle. I've always known she was beautiful, but yesterday when I saw her, in her own bakery, living out her dream I was hit with it all over again. Feelings I've buried for a long time bubbled up to the surface and I forgot why I haven't acted on them for a few minutes. Then Colt called and there was one reason.

"Hey, Rhett." Winnie breaks through my thoughts with her greeting. "What on earth are you doing up and here so early on a Saturday morning?" I take her in. She looks sleepy and adorable. The side of her face is a tiny bit red and swollen. "I'm assuming you were out late last night." She says it in an light but accusing tone.

"Well I was told that getting here early was necessary if I wanted one of these." I hold up the last few bites of the cinnamon roll I just devoured. "....and I went back to the hotel shortly after you tripped on the entry rug." I throw out and fight my smile when I picture it. She relaxes slightly, her tense shoulders lowering the slightest bit.

"Saw that did you? I figured you were a little too busy to notice me with your date sitting next to you." There's a small level of snark detected if I'm not mistaken.

"I don't think anyone missed it, Winnie. You tend to attract some attention." Her cheeks pink at my words. "And she wasn't my date. I had only just met her when you got there last night. Colt invited them there." That seems to put her at ease and I think I like seeing her a little jealous.

"I think you had another hour before that would have been a worry about long lines, but I really appreciate you coming in so early."

"This cinnamon roll was more than worth it." I wink and take another sip of my coffee. She sighs.

"Can I tell you something?"

"Anything." Well that didn't sound desperate. She smiles softly.

"I kind of keep waiting for the other shoe to drop." She says quietly.

"What do you mean? From what I hear, you're killing it." That earns me a wide smile.

"I guess I just worry that this won't last and eventually people will stop coming." Her admission takes me by surprise, not only that she thinks that way but that she would confide in me. She hasn't talked to me like this in years. I've always wanted to know what was going on in her head. I clear my throat.

"You're one of the best people I know, Winnie." She blushes at my words. "There's a reason everyone in this town turns out every day of the week. As amazing as they are, I know for a fact it's not just for the cinnamon rolls or any other baked goods." She averts her gaze.

"Thank you for saying that, Rhett." I laugh.

"I'm not just saying it, it's the truth. You've had everyone we know wrapped around your pretty little finger since you came to town." She rolls her eyes but takes the compliment. Then she meets my gaze.

"The whole town huh?" It's a loaded question. One I'm surprised she doesn't already know the answer to. It's also one I feel like she wouldn't ask if she was with someone.

"I don't know a single person that wouldn't do anything for you." My statement hangs between us feeding into the tension we've let build. I think maybe it's getting too intense for our first conversation alone in years so I add, "I can't go a block without someone telling me how sweet you are. I'm sure Colt has had to give dirty looks to any guy that looks in your direction." It's a cowardly way to ask, but I have to know if she's seeing anyone, who it is, and if it's serious. She laughs outright.

"Oh, you have no idea." Her response gets under my skin and I clear my throat before I ask...

"Anyone serious?" She just looks at me for a handful of seconds before sighing and giving me an answer.

"Mm no. Not as of last night anyway. It didn't really work

out with my boyfriend." She half laughs. "We broke up last night."

"That's too bad." I'm barely containing my relief at this news. On occasion mom or Colt has mentioned she's on a date or out with a boyfriend and I always find myself relieved when I hear it ended. They wouldn't deserve her anyway. She's special. I've known this since I was 15 and mom brought her over to make cookies. Instead of getting sucked into the memory I focus on what she's saying now.

"Eh, it's fine." she waves it off. "I think I need to just be single for a while anyway. Mare thinks I need to try *casual dating*," She scoffs. "I'm not sure I've ever done that."

My heart sinks into my stomach. *Casual* and Winnie do not sound like a combination I'm okay with...she keeps going. "I've always been such a relationship girl. Maybe that's the problem. I guess we'll see." She stands and I can see my time with her dwindling so I rush to put my two cents in.

"There's nothing wrong with wanting to be in a relationship." she huffs a little laugh.

"This coming from you? The serial dater? The 'hockey heartthrob' I've seen so much about? I'm surprised that's your opinion." Yeah I'm not sure why I thought she would take my advice on this subject. Even though I haven't been that guy in years, it's hard to live down a reputation like that. I cringe.

"That was a while ago, Winnie and you can't believe everything you see in articles and on TV." I'm not sure why, but it matters to me that she knows I'm not doing that and haven't been for quite some time.

"Alright, that's true," she says as she takes a couple steps back but I can't tell if she is accepting what I've said. "Thanks again for coming in, Rhett. Support from the new hockey coach is very appreciated." She winks and my heartbeat instantly picks up. Does she know how truly captivating she is?

"You know I'll always support you, Winnie." Her face turns more serious.

"I do know that. Your family has always been there for me and Colt. I'll always be thankful for it. See you around." She's walking through the door that hit her last night and back through the one to my heart. Distracted by that thought, I almost miss the ink on the back of her neck as she slips away. I hadn't noticed it last night.

"See you soon, Winnie," I say into my coffee cup then proceed to buy a danish, cinnamon swirl muffin, and another cinnamon roll because I can't decide on just one. I walk back to the hotel to shower and take a nap before I have to leave for lunch at mom and dads.

I slide the keycard into the door and walk inside. I strip my sweatpants and hoodie and turn the shower on. I'm still thinking about that *casual* comment she made when referring to dating as I step under the spray. I'm not sure I have a right to feel any type of way about that, but I do. Winnie deserves a man who worships the ground she walks on, even if it's not me. I want it to be me.

The one summer I had with her will definitely never be enough. I wanted more then, but she was set on us ending when I started my first year in the NHL that fall. We still talked, I wasn't capable of cutting off communication with her. I called her after practice, and we would watch a movie. Afterwards she would analyze all the characters and I would listen to each one. It was her favorite way to watch a movie and so it became mine.

That only went on for so long before she got busy with

something or hockey season picked up and I got busy with that. She made it to games with my family but I could tell she was putting distance between us. I was too prideful to ask her. Women were throwing themselves at me weekly. I was annoyed that she wasn't also. Ah, I had so much growing up to do.

One summer I came home on a break and Colt told me she was busy. She was busy a lot that summer and continued to be on most of my visits. I didn't ask Colt too many questions because I didn't want him to get the wrong idea...*or the right one more like*, but I asked my mom about Winnie every chance I got. She directed me to go to the source if I had questions about Winnie's life. That didn't feel like something I could do at the time. But now? Now I really just wanted to talk to her.

I think back to Winnie's comment about me being a serial dater and she's not really wrong. I dated a lot over the years. I had one relationship that lasted six months. She came to every game and seemed like the most supportive girlfriend. I remember her being bothered by my friendship with Winnie. Thankfully I realized she wasn't the one and broke things off with her, but she still tried to come around. Kept coming to games and even told a hospital once after we hadn't been together for months that I was her boyfriend.

I felt bad for her until it turned out she was more attracted to just being with an NHL player and it didn't really matter which one. I caught her making out with a guy from an opposing team after being dragged to a bar by my teammates to celebrate a win. I only wish I hadn't wasted so much time on her. After that, I decided I wanted to keep my focus on hockey. No relationships. Talking with Winnie has really made me rethink a lot of the decisions I've made.

I get out of the shower and check the time, lunch isn't until 11:30 and it's only 6:30 now. I lay down letting myself relax and realize I'm even more tired than I thought. So, I set my alarm and let myself drift off thinking about Winnie and her dark hair barely contained with that clip this morning, the tattoo I spotted on the back of her neck, the way she bit her full lower lip, and the bit of flour on her forehead.

RHETT

I ended up making it to mom and dads at 11:45 and am greeted with the front door swinging open before I can turn the handle.

"Rhett!" My baby sister Florence squeals and she jumps into my arms. I half carry, half drag her with me as I walk through the front door.

"Hey, baby Lo. It's so good to see you!" She gives me a tight squeeze then releases me. "When I got to the hotel yesterday, you looked busy with check-ins." I hold her out and look at her. "When did you grow up on me?"

Florence is the baby of the family. A surprise to my parents nine years after having me, she's never wanted for anything in her life. With three older brothers that would do anything for her and parents too old to tell her no, it's a miracle we didn't turn her into a spoiled brat. She's actually turned out to be the sweetest one of us all. She's incredibly smart and driven and has been running the family hotel for two years. In that time she's exceeded expectations and improved on what was already there.

"I'm 23, Rhett," She says like I don't know how old she is. "When are you gonna stop calling me baby Lo?" She's asked this before and I give her the same answer.

"Never. The name stays. Along with all the special treatment from your whole family." We both chuckle because it's true. "Speaking of...where's everybody else?"

"They are all out back, waiting for you to get here." I grin.

"Well I better go make everyone's day then." I wink and Lo rolls her eyes, following me through the house and out the back glass doors to the deck. I see my dad first. He's at the grill talking to mom, making her laugh. She sits on a cushioned chair angled towards dad, holding a glass of wine. The sight makes me grin. Someday I want what they have.

"Hello? I heard you've been waiting on my arrival to get this thing started." Mom whips her head to me and laughs as she stands to give a hug. Dad follows behind her. When he turns I see his apron. *Caution: extremely Hot, and so is the food.* It's one mom got him. He has a whole collection now that we've gifted him over the years. It's so good to see them. They both visited after my injury. Mom even stayed for a couple weeks to help me get settled and take me back and forth to physical therapy.

"Hey son." My dad slaps my back as he pulls me to him. "It's good to have you home. Settle in at the hotel okay?"

"It's really good to be home. Yeah, the hotels fine. I sign the papers on the new house right after I leave here and I'll move in this weekend." His eyebrows raise in surprise.

"Well that was fast. Did you get an inspection? When did you even have time to look at it?"

"I've looked at it plenty of times and I had my agent make sure it was inspected and the report has been gone over multiple times by myself and a professional. Knox looked over it as well as the contract for me, too."

"Huh, he didn't mention anything. Well I'm sure everything is in order if your brother had a hand in it." The comment doesn't bother me like it might have at one point. I know he thinks I'm a capable adult but Knox *is* a lawyer.

"What did I mention and have a hand in?" Knox says as he climbs the stairs to the deck. My adorable, little, two year old niece is high on his hip and he looks at her as he addresses me. "Hi, Uncle Rhett." Hazel smiles so big her nose scrunches and I can see her two tiny teeth. My brother is all but forgotten.

"Hazey! Hi babygirl." I hold my arms out to see if she'll come to me. I've facetimed her weekly since she was born. Knox was annoyed at first but I wanted my niece to know my voice...and I wanted to be her favorite. "Wanna come see Uncle Rhett?" I make my voice as exciting as I can. She wiggles and then nosedives for me. *Yes!*

"That's my girl!" I hug her close then move her to my hip and spin slowly. "I've missed you sweet girl. Have you been making daddy give you everything you want like we talked about?" My dad and Knox both chuckle.

"So what's in order because of me? There is a long list." I shake my head and kiss my niece's cheek.

"You're gonna have to put that guy in his place babygirl," I tell her quietly.

"Rhett's new house," My dad answers.

"I wouldn't say *new*..." Knox says. "It's one of the historical houses in town." My dad looks puzzled.

"You bought a historical house?" Having lived in a luxury

apartment the last six years in Seattle I can see how he might think I would want something newer, but I've loved that house since I was a kid.

"Yeah, it's the one off of Stumbolt," I say as I raise Hazel over my head and blow a raspberry on her belly. She giggles and I feel like I just won the Stanley Cup. I would know what that feels like because I have won it. Three times, but who's counting?

"Off Stumbolt? Isn't that the house that's right down the street from Winnie's place?" Alder asks as he comes out of the house. Hazel squeals and reaches for him. Typical. Alder is always the favorite.

"Hey, Hazel baby! Come see your favorite uncle," he croons. I roll my eyes but pass the little traitor to him after one more smooch to her chubby cheek. Curious about his comment about Winnie. I clear my throat.

"Winnie lives off Stumbolt?" I ask, trying to sound casual.

"Oh yes, she's been working on renovating it. It's darling!" Mom answers while carrying a large bowl of salad and two more plates of food to the table outside.

"I've been over there a few times, helping her carry some tile in and I picked up a couple tools for her because she needed help," Alder adds. "It's looking really nice." I hate that Alder has been in her place and I haven't.

"Dadadada..." Hazel babbles at Knox and her tiny hands make the cutest grabbing motion. He reaches for her and scrunches his nose just like she does and grabs under her arms.

"We better get you inside for a little nap, huh pretty girl?" As if on cue, she yawns. We all wave at her before Knox takes her in, her sweet head resting on his shoulder.

"Hey little brother! 'Bout time you showed up." Alder puts

his arm around my back then swifty slips it up and puts me in a headlock. We wrestle around for a couple minutes before mom shuts it down.

"Boys—if you're going to do that, move it to the yard." Florence snorts.

"And I'm supposed to be the youngest here," she says dryly. I give her a smile then turn to Alder.

"How's everything at the resort?" His comment about Winnie is still on my mind. I didn't know she lived near the house I've had my eye on for the last month. It might make the house even more appealing. For reasons I'm not ready to really dive into.

"It's good. You know how it is in the off season. We're running the lifts right now for the mountain bikers." I nod. Alder works at ski resort a few towns over. He started out as an instructor and now he runs the whole place.

"I need to get out there." My mountain bike hasn't gotten as much use as I would've liked the past couple years but it'll be here with the rest of my things on Monday. "Let me know when a good day is and I'll meet you there."

"Sure, I'll text you Monday and let you know what my weeks looking like. It's gonna be nice to have you back here to ride with. Knox hardly does anything anymore."

"Knox has a child." My mom fixes him with a look. He rushes to add.

"...because he's busy taking care of my perfect niece." She smiles at him then and I chuckle. We will never be too old to be put in our place by her.

"Alright family! We are ready to eat, everyone to the table!" Dad announces.

We all make our way to our seats and start piling our plates high. Knox walks out with a baby monitor and sets it on the table. A sleeping Hazel on the screen. I've missed this. Having lunch on a random Friday with my family. I look around the table and feel incredibly grateful and fortunate to have these people in my life.

After lunch everyone helps mom bring in the dishes to the kitchen. We say our goodbyes and it's nice to know that it won't be months or even weeks before I'm able to do this again. I give mom and dad another hug and head to the school. I'm meeting my team for the first time today and getting them on a schedule and talk to them about their participation in the festival happening tomorrow. When I was asked if the hockey team would have a booth a month ago, I said yes automatically and sent out an email to the list the school provided to ask the boys to come up with a theme.

Their ideas ranged from "magic mike" to "jello wrestling" but when I shot those down I allowed "kissing booth". I shake my head. I said yes because it sounded like something I would have done. I have a feeling these boys are going to be a handful. I will also be stopping by the title company to sign papers to make the house on Stumbolt officially mine. The thought makes me smile and I'm genuinely excited to slow down and settle in here.

WINNIE

I'm exhausted and a little punchy. I've been here at Thistle and Sage since way too early this morning working on all the food for the festival tomorrow. Anna took care of everything we needed in the shop today so I could focus on tomorrow. She has a real knack for baking and is going to start helping me out in the kitchen more. I let her go at four so she could get some rest before working in the booth all day with me tomorrow.

I let out a long and tired sigh and swipe the loose hair out of my face. It's been a long day. I've had that thought most days over the last four months, but after the events of last night and this morning I can feel my anxiety bubbling near the surface and keeping it at bay is really zapping my energy.

I finish wiping down the counters and grab my things to go. I feel my phone vibrate in my back pocket and pull it out to see Mare is calling me. Probably to check in on me. I haven't had a chance to update her on Rhett being back in town. She's the only one who knows about what happened four years ago.

"Aren't you supposed to be working until 8 tonight?" I ask when I tap the screen to answer.

"I am, but I'm between surgeries so I wanted to call and check on you. I also have to tell you something." I frown. That usually comes with either bad news or gossip and her tone isn't very gossipy. I lock the front door and start my walk home.

"I'm fine. Really. It was a shock but it was for the best. I really don't think I could have listened to him talk about his peach crop one more time. He made it sound dirty..." I shiver. "Anyway, what do you have to tell me?" She laughs.

"He did talk about peaches a little too sensually."

"Entirely too much." I laugh with her. "Now what's the thing?"

"Well I'm not sure how you'll react but I heard a couple of the nurses talking this morning and they were talking about Rhett." She pauses. "I guess he's back in town..." She trails off.

"Yeah, I know." I think about his twinkling eyes last night and our short conversation. "I guess he's taking over for Coach Reynolds at the high school," I inform her.

"What? When did you find this out and why didn't you tell me?"

"I just found out last night after we got off the phone."

"Did Colt tell you?" I roll my eyes.

"Colt? Why would he tell me? He has no idea that I would even care." I grumble. "Not that I do," I add.

"Oh knock that shit off, Win. It's me." I sigh.

"I shouldn't care. I didn't think I did anymore. Then I saw him."

"Wait. You saw him? Where?"

"Listen, last night was a long one." I continue to tell her all about our encounter last night. She laughs a little too hard when I tell her I'm sporting a bruise on the side of my face from the swinging door.

"So, he's back for good then?" she asks me as I turn the corner to my house. There's no car parked in front of the Miller's' house tonight and I'm grateful. It's been for sale for a little over a month and there has been a lot of foot traffic. I'm not a huge fan of change, I really don't like when I have zero control over said change. Like my new neighbor. I just hope whoever it is turns out to be nice. The Millers were elderly and had a golden retriever that I loved. They would sit outside and talk to me while I worked in my garden or on something for the house. There was always something to do and never enough time to do it.

"I mean, he made it sound that way, but who knows?" I'm on my front porch now and turning my key in the door.

"I'll see what else I can get out of the nurses." I laugh at that.

"Don't scare them too bad." She scoffs.

"Me? Scare them?" I laugh harder at that. I hear the click and push it open. I can feel my shoulders relax as I walk into my home. I've turned this space into my safe haven. My sweet little cottage is still a work in progress, but so am I. Seeing the potential shine through even when it's covered in a layer of 'geese wearing bonnets' wallpaper is a metaphor I like to apply to myself. Working on this place has become a form of therapy for me.

"So, we're on for next weekend? You'll come out with me?"

"Yes. I may regret it but I think I need to get out. Meet someone." She gasps.

"Winnie Parker. Are you looking for a one night stand?"

"I didn't say that...but maybe...? I don't know." She giggles.

"Well you don't have to decide right now." I consider that.

"True. I downloaded my dating app."

"You did? When? You just broke up with Sam last night...oh..."

"Oh? Oh, what?" She chuckles softly.

"You are still into him." My face screws up on it's own.

"Sam? I think I was already over him when everything went down last night."

"Not Sam, Winnie." Oh, *that him*.

"Then who?" I know exactly who she's referring to, but I don't want to admit it. It's been a long road to recovery and one slip may have me back under the spell that is Rhett Holloway.

"Fine. We won't talk about it."

"There's nothing to talk about, Mare." I look down at my shirt. "Uhg, hold on. I'm a mess." I have various baking ingredients all over me so as I'm passing through the kitchen on my way to the laundry room I tap the speaker icon and set my phone down and pull my shirt over my head.

"Just know whenever you want to talk about it, I'm here. No judgment," she offers. I lean back against the sink and contemplate telling her how terrible it was that it wasn't terrible to see him. How when he put his hand to my cheek, my stomach flipped like there was a full on cirque du soleil performance going on in there.

"I know you are. Thank you and I love you. It'd been a long time and regardless of if I'm over him or not, I'm sure he's moved on from me. I've seen it." I hear a beeping and shuffling.

"My pager just went off, I have to go, but I'll see you

tomorrow at the festival! Make sure you hydrate! Night, Win. Please text me or call if you need me."

"I will. Thanks for the reminder. Night, Mare. Go be a badass!" I can hear the smirk in her voice when she replies.

"When am I not?" I laugh and tap my screen. I turn and decide I probably should hydrate. I'm not good at remembering to drink enough water during the day. I always end up drinking so much at night that I have to get out of bed at night to pee. I reach for a glass on one of my open shelves that I installed myself.

Only when I'm reaching for my glass, I notice that there's a light on in the house across the way. Huh, someone must have left it on when they showed it today. I feel my head cock to the side. I squint my eyes to get a better look and rear back when I realize there's someone standing at the window. I shriek and drop to my kitchen floor. The cold floor reminds me that I'm still shirtless and chose to wear a black lacy bralette this morning, because I need to do laundry. Whoever is over there just got a free show tonight. I lay on the floor for a few minutes and cover my face with my hands, mortified.

I'm not one to be ashamed of my body or shy away from a bit of skin, but for all I know the little old man moving in next door now thinks his neighbor is a lady of the night, trying to seduce him away from his wife. I laugh a little at how ridiculous that sounds and feel a little better. They probably couldn't see very clearly anyway.

On the other hand, if they did happen to see me, I don't think I can stand up. What if that's my new neighbor? On the off chance they are still standing there, I slowly crawl on my hands and knees into my laundry room. I'm just clear of the kitchen windows when I hear my doorbell. *No.* I whine. Surely this is not the person that just saw me shirtless. Do I have to answer? My doorbell chimes for the second time. *Again?* I throw on the first thing I find—a faded old comfort sweatshirt. I stand and stumble through the house to the front window to see who's ringing my doorbell, praying it's not the person that just got the free show.

RHETT

I'm walking around my new house. It's everything I was looking for when I thought about settling in here. The massive staircase. Tall ceilings. Large kitchen. Four bedrooms and an office. An enclosed sunroom out back. The yard is amazing, with a patio for having friends and family over. It needs some updating but I want to keep the integrity intact.

I look out the big window in the living room and see Winnie. She looks adorable. Messy. It makes me smile. She must be walking home from work. My family mentioned she lived close by. I feel a little like a stalker as I walk through the house to keep her in frame. I'm surprised when I see her open the gate and walk into the cottage right next door. I knew we would be living on the same street but I had no idea she would be this close. I feel my lips turn up. *We're neighbors.*

I take the stairs up two at a time remembering to grab my keys I left on the bathroom counter. The rest of my things should be here Sunday, which is probably when Winnie will find out I'm living next door. I wonder how she'll react. While

I've been thinking about her over the years, she could have been forgetting everything we shared all those years ago. That thought is foreign to me. There's absolutely no way I could forget anything about her. I smile thinking about the summer I had no idea would be my undoing.

It was just two weeks after I turned 25. I had just been drafted into the NHL. In three months, I would be moving to Seattle to start my hockey career. Before my life got too busy, I was home visiting for the summer and we were celebrating with a camping trip up in the mountains. It was supposed to be a small group of us but with Colt involved things got out of control pretty quickly.

More people were still showing up to our campsite and there was too much beer floating around. I had plenty of other people to focus on, but there was only one person I could be bothered to look at. Unfortunately for me, I wasn't the only one looking. Winnie had always been beautiful. That was just a fact that existed in the world. Like the sun rising in the east and setting in the west. There was gravity and Winnie was beautiful.

I watched as she flitted from boy to boy most of the night, smiling sweetly, but politely declining drinks. If you didn't know her you would think she was having a good time—I knew different. I could tell by the tightness in her shoulders and the way she kept touching her right temple that she was getting anxious, yet it still drove me crazy she was willing to give her attention to everyone but me. Against my better judgment, I was about to go ask if she wanted to take a walk when I saw her excuse herself from one of the drunk idiots hanging all over her and head towards the lake. Following her was a bad idea. I wasn't always full of good ones.

I told myself that trailing after her was just to make sure no one else did, but that excuse was flimsy at best. The truth was I wanted to be near her. To talk to her. I had missed her while I was away at school, no one makes me laugh the way she does. I watch her climb over a large rock at the waters edge and let her feet dip into the lake. Watch her visibly relax under the moon. She tilts her head back and her hair falls down her back. I've never wished to be anything other than what I am but I wished I were an artist so I could paint her in this moment and have it forever. I take a step forward, not sure what to say and hear a branch snap under my foot. She whips her head around and stares at me with wide eyes that turn threatening when she sees it's me. She looks so vicious I can't help the nickname that comes out.

"Hey, honeybee." She rolls those pretty melted honey eyes and my lips twitch.

"Rhett? What are you doing out here? Shouldn't you be back at the bonfire with your adoring fans?" I can't hide my smile now. She must have really needed to some alone time. She's snapping at me. I decide to swat back at her.

"Jealous, honeybee?" I've caught her staring at me plenty of times over the years. She backed off when she got a boyfriend at 17. I wanted to tell him to get lost but that wasn't really fair of me if I wasn't planning to do anything about it. Tonight though, I felt differently. She gives me a flat look but I think I see her tense a little before I go on. "I figured I would let Colt have a turn. He's not one to get jealous, but he did invite most of the people here." She snorts.

"How very generous of you." My smile widens after she turns her head back to the lake. Not giving me a second glance. I'm moving toward her then, helpless to the pull.

"So what are you doing out here alone? Where's Marigold?" I ask her as I settle beside her on the flat rock she's camped on. She sighs before answering me.

"It's just really loud—and I don't know more people than I do." I study her profile, the freckles across her upturned nose are barely visible in the moonlight.

"It is really loud, I guess it doesn't bother me as much since I'm in used to-..."

"If you say '*your screaming fans*', Rhett Holloway..." She cuts me off with the threat, her finger pointed at my chest. The look on her face is serious but I can see the shine in her eyes and even though I've looked at her all night, having her face this close to mine has my chest warming. I grab her hand and pull her closer. Her breath catches. The part of my brain that makes decisions is impaired and it's not from the alcohol.

"That's not what I was going to say," I say quietly. Her hand in mine is drowning out the voice in the back of my head reminding me that this is Colt's sister. She looks at our hands and then back up to my face. I'm not sure what she sees there but her brows pull together and she looks so adorable I can't take it. I let my other hand slide up her bare arm and feel goose-bumps rise before I tangle my fingers in the curls at her neck and lean closer.

"Rhett...?" My name is a question and I can taste it in the air.

"Yes, Winnie?" I run my nose up the side of her cheek. My mind is empty except for one thought that plays on loop...*please don't push me away*. She swallows.

"Are you going to kiss me?" *Oh, thank God.* I brush my mouth against hers gently once, then twice. I'm trying to hold back and go slow. I don't want to overstimulate her, I want her to enjoy this.

"Rhett?" she whispers again. *Oh no, I've already ruined it.*

"Yes, Winnie?" I wait for her to tell me that this isn't what she wants and how bad her rejection is going to feel. Her answer sealed my fate. Solidified that I would follow this woman anywhere. Anything she wanted, I would give.

"When I asked if you were going to kiss me I meant really kiss me."

I laugh quietly in the empty bedroom upstairs and run my thumb over my bottom lip. I'm getting ready to relive mine and Winnie's first real kiss when a light out the window catches my attention. My favorite thing about it is that the master bedroom is the big window on the back of the house that I'm now real-izing faces Winnie's cottage. I can see right into Winnie's kitchen, which is probably her favorite thing about her place. That thought makes me smile.

She's always been good in the kitchen. In so many of my memories of her she's helping mom in the kitchen with dinner or baking something for dessert. I'm so proud of her. I just wish I could have talked to her more over the years. I see her standing in the window and at first I think she might be facing me. I am proven wrong as she turns and reaches for something high, stops and gives me a torturously long look at so much of her bare skin and black lace covering very little of it. I gulp and before I can stop myself I —*wave? No. I did not just wave at her like some creepy pervert.*

I see her form drop from view. Oh, God, she probably

thinks I'm some stalker—she's not totally wrong in thinking that. I was being stalkery. I need to go tell her it was just me. I rush down the stairs, almost tripping and falling down the last five. I don't even bother with my shoes as I jog down the sidewalk to her gate, jump it and make it onto the porch. I ring her doorbell and wait. I ring it again. There's a small commotion inside, a curse that has me pinching my lips together so my laugh won't escape.

I see motion to my left and see the blinds on the window move then more cursing and footsteps. The door flying open has me taking a step back, I'm not prepared for the sight before me. I scan her flushed face and her haphazardly pulled up hair with little pieces escaping all over. She's so adorable I can hardly stand it—but what has my full attention is the faded sweatshirt that's swallowing her. *It's mine.*

"Rhett? What are you doing here?" She pops her head out and looks from side to side as if to see if the coast is clear.

"Well I figured I should come over and explain."

"Explain what? How do you even know where I live?" She shifts her weight to the side, leaning against the door frame and crosses her arms. Defensive. Great.

"Well, I wanted you to know that I wasn't staring at you or spying on you. I just happened to be upstairs when—well when I noticed the light on—and then I noticed you didn't have any—"

"Wait! That was *you* next door?!" she cuts off my stammering which I'm grateful for. I just nod. Her head tilts to the side as she stares at me, eyes swimming with questions. The flush that stained her cheeks a few moments ago is now spreading down her delicate neck.

"Uh, yeah. I just signed the papers today." I give her a grin I know she used to love. She blinks.

"Signed the papers? On what?" She asks the questions slowly. I roll my eyes.

"The house, Winnie. I'm moving in this weekend."

"You're kidding. I didn't even know it sold." Her arms loosen to her sides and she puts a hand on her cocked hip. We're getting somewhere.

"It did..." I grin at her again. "Hey, neighbor." She makes a little *hmph* sound.

"So, you're really planning on sticking around then?" Now it's my turn to be confused.

"Of course. I told you I took the coaching job at the school." She bobs her head.

"Yeah, I know. It's just surprising that you would stay after being gone for so long." Her tone is accusing and I'm more than a little thrown off by it.

"It's always been the plan to come back. You know that. I told you that." Her eyes meet mine then and something flickers there between us but it's gone before I can name it.

"That's great. Like I said at the bakery, your family has really missed you. I better head in now. I have to be up early for the festival in the morning. I guess I'll be seeing you—neighbor." She smirks and goes to shut the door. I turn to leave but can't stop from teasing her.

"Night, Winnie. You look great by the way." She rolls her eyes and opens her mouth with what I'm sure is a witty retort but I'm not done. "In my old sweatshirt—and out of it." I wink and her eyes bulge before she looks down at her body, throwing her arms over her chest again. I chuckle the whole way home.

WINNIE

The day has flown by. I'm sweating and the fan that's set up in the corner of my booth is doing nothing but blowing more hot air directly into me. It's these late days of summer that have you wearing your sweater in the mornings and thanking God you wore a tank top under it in the afternoon. I also may still be blushing over Rhett's impromptu visit last night. I wanted to die when I remembered what sweatshirt I had on. I catch myself biting at my thumbnail and pull my hand away from my face, another anxious habit I'm perpetually trying to break.

There are still a few hours left of the festival before I can clean up. I let Anna go a half hour ago when her friends stopped by to visit. She gave me a half hearted '*Are you sure?*' before flinging her apron at me and bounding off, giggling with the group of girls. It's just me now but luckily it's slowing down. Which is good because I only have a few items left.

"Winnie!" I look up to see Mary Holloway coming towards me.

"Hi, Mary!" I smile and wave.

"Would you look at that...you barely have anything left."

"I know. I can't believe it."

"I can." She gives me a knowing smile. "You're so talented, sweetie." I beam at her.

"Thank you, Mary. It means the most coming from you."

"Have you had a chance to walk around yet? Rhett's team is having a hay day at their kissing booth." She chuckles.

"A kissing booth, huh?" I should be surprised but it's the most on brand thing Rhett could do. "I haven't had a chance yet. I need to stop by Uncle Bucks, too. I'm starving and some chili and a beer sounds pretty good." She steps around my makeshift counter and comes to stand beside me. I give her a puzzled look.

"Well go on then. I can man your booth for a bit. I've seen it all." She winks and me and I give her a hug.

"You know why I love these events so much?"

"Why? And don't tell me it's because Sue Anderson gets tipsy at each one and starts spilling the not so secret things her and Bradley get up to." She shudders and I burst out laughing.

"If I'm being completely honest I don't hate that, it's always been really informative, but no. It's because of you, Mary." She cocks her head to the side and purses her lips, so I go on. "You took me around at my very first event here in town and gave me this." I hold up my wrist to show her the bracelet she gave me 17 years ago. "You gave me this and it made me feel so special— like maybe I would be okay eventually. I hadn't felt like that in months."

"Oh, sweetheart." She pulls me back into a hug. "I have loved you as my own daughter all these years and I always will." My eyes well but I hold back the tears. Mary Holloway has been a pillar in my upbringing.

"I know. I love you, too."

"Now go have some fun out there!" She shoo's me. "And if you see Rhett, will you tell him we're having family lunch tomorrow at 11:30? Will you come?"

"Of course. I would love to." I'm not sure how I feel about spending so much time with Rhett. I'm also not sure how I'm going to avoid it. His fence is also my fence.

"Good. I'll be here and can close it down for you. Tom's around here somewhere and I'll enlist his help later."

"You don't have to do that! I'll be back—"

"Please just go be young and carefree for awhile." She cuts off my protest.

"Alright, I will. But please call if you need anything!" I smile.

"Bye, sweetie!"

"Bye, Mary." I go straight to my uncle's booth first, I wasn't kidding when I said I was starving. He's waving his hands around in the air, entertaining a group as usual. Uncle Buck has never shied away from the spotlight. A trait I really admire. He's never nervous in a crowd, he'll have them laughing and at ease in a matter of moments. Colt's like that. Me, not so much. I love being around *my* people, but new people, lots of new people. Count me out, better yet, don't count me at all. He spots me as he waves those animated hands again and winks at me. I grin and give a tiny wave before securing my spot in line for chili. He finishes his story and says goodbye to his new friends then motions for me to come over. I shake my head, but my stomach growls, so I find myself making the decision to slip out of line and taking advantage of family benefits.

"Winnie!" I smile at his excitement in seeing me.

"Hey, Uncle Buck. Looks like you've been pretty busy over here." He grins.

"You know me, always in for a good story." I grin back at him. I feel a hand clamp onto my shoulder and then something wet soaks into my side.

"Baby sister!" Colt greets me loudly and squeezes me until I come off the ground.

"Colt! You're wet, stop it!" He sets me down but keeps his arm slung over my shoulder.

"I came straight from my last run. Didn't want to miss family dinner." He winks. Yes, if there's one thing my brother has in spades. It's charm and he comes by it honest. Our dad was the same way. A small pang as the thought makes my stomach twinge, but I smile. He looks so much like him, from what I can remember. Things are getting a little fuzzy in my head. I clear my throat.

"How was the water today?" He looks out towards the mountains and smiles wide.

"Perfect." I roll my eyes.

"Oh really? Because you say that every time I ask."

"That's because it's always perfect. Wouldn't change a thing." An easy smile is on his face. He's good at making things look easy. I don't envy my brother in too many ways, his struggles are not something I have to contend with but this is one of the times I do. He's wild in a way I never will be. Too much can go wrong in the wilderness and even though Colt is certified in as many things as you can be to guide rafts all day and be out there—I'm still going to worry. Uncle Buck sets two bowls of chili down on the counter in front of us and reaches to the side to grab a couple spoons for us, handing one to my brother. He accepts it and we dig in.

Colts almost finished with his when two plastic cups of beer appear next to our bowls.

"Ah, yes. Thank you, Uncle Buck. This is exactly what I needed." I thank him.

"No need to thank me, sweetheart. It's just good to see you two." I smile.

"You, too. Dinner on Wednesday?"

"You know it, I'm making spaghetti and meatballs." He says proudly and I laugh because it's always what he makes.

"Ahh...just what I needed to refuel after being in a boat all day." Colt chimes in, he's guzzled his beer and wipes his mouth with his napkin before kissing the top of my head as he stands.

"Love you, Win. It's been fun, fam, but I've got a date. See you Wednesday!" He tosses his plate and cup into the trash bin.

"You're going in your wet clothes?"

"She won't be worried about my wet clothes." He waggles his eyebrows and I smile at his unwavering confidence.

"See you Wednesday, love you." He disappears into the crowd. I stand and throw my bowl away, I still have half of my beer. Uncle Buck is talking to Jay, one of his servers.

"I'm going to walk around." I mouth to my uncle. "Love you." he smiles and calls "Love you, Win!" I walk in the direction of the cotton candy machine. I won't consider this a successful fair until I've had some.

I'm walking with a giant pink fluffy cloud on a stick when I see Rhett's booth. Or his teams. I scan the spaces surrounding them, but I don't see him. There is still a very long line of high school girls waiting for a chance to kiss a hockey player. I sigh. I can sympathize. It doesn't feel so long ago that I would have stood in a line all night for a chance at kissing Rhett.

"Winnie." I jump and look to my right, mouth full of melting pink sugar.

"Rhett. Jeeze you scared me. What are you doing over here?" He smiles and holds up his hand showing me a pink fluffy cloud of his own.

"It's not a successful fair unless I get some cotton candy." I blink hearing his words echo my thoughts from earlier. I swallow and nod in agreement.

"Mhmm...well I'm also supposed to tell you there's family lunch tomorrow."

"Is there now? And you volunteered to relay this information?" He pulls a piece of the sticky sugar from the rest and pops it into his mouth.

"Your mom asked me to tell you if I saw you." I say as blandly as I can. "I saw you."

"I saw you, too, looking around a few minutes ago. Thought you may have been looking for someone." His tone is overly innocent and my blush has returned.

"Nope, just checking out the crowd. It looks like your booth is doing well." He smiles at me, knowingly.

"Yeah, it's going pretty well. You know, lunch at my parents tomorrow is going to put a kink in my plans."

"You have plans? A lunch date?" His dimples are on full display now.

"Kind of. I was really looking forward to getting to know my new neighbor." I feel my mouth pop open. Is he flirting with me? "Last night, I didn't really get a good look at her, but from what I could tell. Absolute smokeshow." Well that answers my question, just not why—maybe I don't care right now. I tuck my hair behind my ear and look up at him through my lashes.

"Well you are in luck then because...I was also invited." I say as I take another nibble of my cotton candy. His eyes brighten, crinkling at the corners showing me his panty dropping smile. His hand comes up and with his thumb he swipes some stray melted sugar from just under my bottom lip. I stop breathing.

"Perfect." He starts to say something else but a loud gasp from the crowd has us turning towards the boys.

"That didn't sound good." I say looking over to the crowd. Oh no.

"No. It didn't." His tone is only slightly annoyed before he looks back to look me in the eyes. "To be continued." He stalks off towards a high schooler whose pants are pulled down, mooning the large group of onlookers. I cover my mouth to try and smother my laugh. I cannot wait to see how Rhett handles this. He stands in front of the boy with his head slightly bowed and says something quietly. The boy pulls his pants up and stops smiling. Rhett points in a direction away from the crowd and the boy starts walking that way with his head hung low. Rhett looks back at me and I'm guessing my expression is not as stern as it should be because he gives me a reproachful look and shakes his head at me too. I put on a my most apologetic look, mouthing "*Sorry, Coach*" and his eyes spark at the sentiment. I laugh and turn to leave so he can handle his situation.

I stop at one of the local breweries booths and get another beer. It's slowing down and people are starting to gather at the other side of the festival to claim their spots before the fireworks start tonight. I'm walking back to my booth to make sure

Mary and Tom don't need me to help pack up and when they tell me they've got it covered I walk home.

It's only later when I'm sitting on my front porch watching the fireworks that I think about my conversation with Rhett. Flirting with him seems harmless enough on the surface, but I know how bad it will be when it ends. And it will end. One day when he decides he wants more than what I can give, he'll walk away and take whatever love I've allowed myself to have with him.

WINNIE

I saw the moving truck in front of the house next door this morning, Rhett's house now. It's going to take some time to get used to the fact that he's going to be my neighbor. I've touched the spot where he did with his thumb more times than I care to admit in the last 10 hours. I shake off the temptation to do it again and turn towards my oven when the timer goes off. I take out the baking dish, setting it next to the other dishes I'm taking today. I'm bringing a dozen cinnamon rolls, a chocolate raspberry cake, and two loaves of bread. I owe so much to Tom and Mary. I always like to pay them back, even in some small way, whenever I can. Baked goods are also my love language. I have a ball cap that says just that to prove it. I chuckle to myself remembering the gift from Mare when I opened the bakery.

I check the clock and it's 10:15. Mary said 11:30, so I don't have any extra time. I rush through my shower and throw on one of my sundresses. I like this one. It's white with little yellow daisies all over it. It hangs past my knees but has a cute slit up the left leg. I decide to fill my brows and put on mascara, and add some chapstick. I apply lots of product to my wet hair then brush it out, add more and scrunch it slightly and there's just enough time to diffuse it. Curly hair is a process and I haven't been taking care of mine very well lately. Maybe I'll see if Mare wants to do hair masks tomorrow night since we're going out for my birthday this weekend. She was on call last night so she still hasn't answered my previous four texts.

Once my hair is just about dry I call it good. Spritz myself with my favorite perfume and lace up my sneakers. I walk out onto my porch with my arms full of food that I have to set down to lock up. When I turn around Rhett's truck is pulling up. What is he doing here? He gets out and comes up my walkway.

"Hey...what are you doing here?" He smiles and my heart pounds. Will that ever go away? I hope so. He clears his throat as he takes my front steps two at a time.

"I just thought you might want a ride. We're both going to the same place." He picks up the tote bags of food from the porch. "Are those cinnamon rolls?!" he looks so excited. I giggle and his head snaps up. He just stares at my face, up to my hair, then down my body till he gets to the slit in my dress that exposes my leg. He visibly swallows and I blush.

"They are." Why does my voice sound like that? All breathy? I inwardly cringe.

"Alright, let's get going. Tom and Mary are easy going but they do like to start family lunches on time." I smile.

"I know. I've only ever been late to something once, it was not something I care to repeat." He laughs and leads me to the truck.

"Oh please. Like you couldn't get away with anything..." he opens my door and I climb in.

"I have no idea what you're referring to." I smile as sweetly as I can. "I follow the same rules as anyone else." He scoffs, swings the door shut, puts the totes in the backseat then leans in through the open window.

"That's not even close to the truth and you know it. You've always had everyone under your spell."

"Oh, so now I'm a witch?" I call as he's walking to the driver's side. I really wish that were the case. If it was, I would have cast a spell over myself. One that lifts the thoughts of losing those I love. I would have been waiting for Rhett on the porch today. He would have pulled me in for a kiss when he saw me. Told me he missed me even though it had only been a few hours and I wouldn't have wanted to run. But that's not my reality. I had to face that years ago when I thought Rhett and I may have had a shot. Loving someone, no matter how much, only hurts double that amount when it ends. That thought sobers me. It helps ground me. Rhett Holloway may be flirting with me but he won't be wrapped around my little finger forever. He'll get tired of the distance I'll continue to put between us. I'm just cursed to fall for him again and again.

"Winnie...where'd you go?" I blink. Great, how long have I been sitting in silence feeling sorry for myself?

"Sorry, I just get lost in my own head sometimes."

"I know. I feel like you live a completely different life in that pretty head of yours." I do my best to ignore the *pretty* part of that sentence, but it still sends butterflies loose in my stomach.

"Sorry, I'm sure it's annoying to have to sit in silence while I'm doing that." I could not be any more embarrassed. Kill me. He shakes his head adamantly.

"Don't be sorry, honeybee—just take me with you next

time." He winks and my heart feels like it could burst. No one has ever made me feel special the way he does. Maybe I should stop comparing everyone I date to him. I'm not saying Sam was right or validated in what he did to me, but I am saying he could most likely tell I wasn't ever fully invested. Maybe he could even feel that I wasn't ever going to be. He should have ended it with me before moving on with someone else but I shouldn't have kept forcing it with him when it wasn't going to work out.

"You're leaving me behind again." There's a smile in his voice. "What's going on in there?"

"Uhm...I was actually thinking about Sam."

"That jerk? Why?" His reaction takes me by surprise.

"Why would you think he was a jerk?" Guess word about my breakup has started making the rounds.

"He cheated on you, Winnie. You." He swings his hand toward me to drive the point home. "So, not only is he an idiot, but also a huge jerk." There's my confirmation.

I snort and try to brush off his compliment.

"You sound just like Colt. You guys are so overprotective." He looks over at me then and slows the truck.

"I'm not saying that just because I'm protective of you. I am, but also I'm saying that as a man with eyes. He's absolutely an idiot if he can't see you, Winnie." I blush again and try to remain here on earth because it's really hard not to float away when he says things like that to me.

"Thanks, Rhett. That's really sweet to say and I appreciate it." He doesn't seem accepting of my response but we're here at his parents now so I open my door and get out. Feeling like I'm on a cloud and also like I have one hanging over my head I go to get the totes but Rhett stops me.

"Ah, ah, I got it. Head on in, I'll be right behind you."

"Thanks." A squeal tears through the air and I turn to see Florence holding Hazel on her hip.

"Hazyyy!" I'm running up to her and she is squeezing her little hands into fists and babbling. "Hi, sweet girl. It is so good to see you." I pluck her from Florence and spin her in a circle. High pitched shrieks sound and I dance back and forth with her on my hip. I smell her chestnut baby curl covered head. "I've missed you so much babygirl." Knox steps out the front door then and smiles.

"Hey, Winnie."

"Hey, Knox. Gosh she looks bigger."

"Growing way too fast but it kinda makes me proud at the same time. Being a parent is weird." He looks past my shoulder, smiles wide, then steps closer and puts his arm around me. "It's really good to see you. You look beautiful today."

"Uh... thanks, Knox." I take in his suit. "You look nice, too."

"Alright, let's get inside. I'm sure mom and dad are waiting." Rhett bumps his shoulder into Knox's when he passes and Knox lets out a chuckle and follows him in. What was that about? I walk in with Hazel on my hip and her grabbing handfuls of my wild hair.

"Winnie! Oh, sweetie, it's been too long since you've been over. I know you're busy but I need to see you more." I smile warmly at Mary. I love her so much.

"I need to see you more, too. Let's get lunch next week." Hazel nosedives toward the floor so I guess she's done being held. I put her down and she teeters off towards Alder. He makes eye contact with me, smiles his big adorable smile, then crouches down to talk to his niece.

"Yes! And I think you need to start coming for weekly

family dinners again. I know you're busy with the bakery. Have I mentioned how incredibly proud of you we are by the way?" My eyes sting. I was robbed of the chance to share any of my successes with my mom way too young, but Mary has always been like another mother to me. I swallow against the lump.

"You have and thank you. I wouldn't be doing any of this without you and Tom." She waves me off.

"You would have been thriving no matter what, Winnie. That's just how you're built." Now it's my turn to wave her off.

"So, what's for dinner? Can I help?"

"Tom is grilling steaks out back and I already have a salad made up and Knox made brussel sprouts with balsamic and bacon. You just go out back, grab a drink and relax. You've been working so much lately."

"Okay, let me know if you change your mind." I walk out onto the deck and see Knox and Rhett throwing a football. I go over to the grill where Tom is turning over steaks.

"Hey, Winnie. How's it going sweetheart?" I kiss his cheek.

"Going good. Busy...but busy is good."

"That's right. I've heard from multiple people that you're really doing a great job. Everyone's talking about your bakery." I flush at the compliment.

"Well it's like I told Mary, you guys have been there every step of the way and I couldn't have done any of this without you both." He shrugs.

"You've always been smart and driven, Winnie. You were always going to do something amazing with your life." I smile. Tom and Mary Holloway are very different in so many ways but they are so similar in the ways that count.

"Thank you."

"No thanks, needed." He winks and it reminds me so much of Rhett.

"Alright!" He calls out to everyone. "Let's eat!" We all make our way to the table and I find my seat. Alder sits next to me on the right and Florence makes to sit on my other side and I smile at her but then her smile turns knowing and I follow her form to where she sits across from me. Confused, I look to my other side and see that Rhett has claimed that seat. Hmm... okay. He doesn't usually sit next to me at these things... although Colt isn't here today.

"So, any plans for your birthday, Winnie?" Alder draws my attention to him while putting salad on his plate.

"Uhm...sort of. Nothing crazy. Mare wants to take me out for dinner and then get drinks at Uncle Bucks."

"That sounds fun. Can I come?" I smile and hear Rhett groan on my other side.

"Of course. We're planning for dinner at 7."

"I'll be there." Alder Holloway is gorgeous. His dark brown hair paired with twinkling blue eyes brimming with flirty comments is pretty undeniable. All the Holloway boys are beautiful and I'm not the only one who thinks so—but it's Rhett who's always had my attention. His gemstone eyes and shaggy dark hair. He's more than a foot taller than me and all broad shoulders and muscled thighs. The tattoos on his forearm just accentuate the way their strength and the dimples that appear when he grins always leave me a little dazed. The effect he has on me is something I hoped would fade after all these years.

It was better when I wasn't seeing him, now that he's back in town for good, it's likely I would see him often, not everyday, but he's going to be my neighbor. I'm not sure how to get over him. I know what Mare would say. She has said it and I'm starting to think that maybe she's got the right idea. Obviously Sam wasn't the right choice. Not only did he cheat on me but there was never a spark. No heat...not even a sizzle. I wasn't attracted to him despite him being a very attractive man. I sigh and Rhett looks over at me.

"You okay?" he mouths the words, not drawing any one else's attention. I just smile and nod. When will I stop being a complete weirdo around this man? Probably when I stop wanting to crawl into his lap and kiss him...so that answers that. Never. Lunch passes with only a few minor arguments between siblings. Colt and I have never really fought over anything so I love being around all the Holloway kids. They fight but they also would do anything for one another. That part Colt and I have down. I'm hugging Mary and deciding on when to get lunch when Rhett tugs me into the entryway by my elbow.

"You ready to go?" I laugh.

"I'm sensing you are—just let me grab those tote bags."

"I already have them in the truck along with four of those cinnamon rolls to take with me."

"Four?!" He puts his hand over my mouth.

"Shh...I snuck them out. Now let's do the same because I don't want to share anymore today." He says it like it's more than the cinnamon rolls. I know better but I like hearing he doesn't want to share me either.

"Bye everyone!" I get scattered goodbye's and drop a kiss on Hazel's plump little cheek as we pass by and out of the house. As I do, Knox kisses the top of my head. Before I can question what that was about I'm being carried towards the truck and Knox is laughing like a hyena. Rhett opens my door and lifts me into the seat.

"Whoa...where's the fire, cowboy?" His green eyes connect with mine and I start giggling at how serious this man looks right now. "I can get myself in, thank you." He huffs but just shuts my door and walks around the front of the truck. He's pouting and I can't help but tease him.

"So, what's the hurry to get back? Um...do you have plans?"

"What? No, I don't have plans." His jaw ticks so I know there's more. I wait. "I just figured you'd want to get out of there so my brothers could quit drooling all over you."

I laugh loudly but when he isn't laughing with me I see the serious look on his face.

"Oh, Rhett come on. Be serious."

"I am. Alder had to sit right next to you..."

"You sat next to me..." I cut in.

"...and Knox couldn't keep his hands...or his lips to himself..." I burst out again and this time I see the corner of his mouth tip up.

"If I didn't know any better. I would think you were a little jealous, Rhett." I'm teasing him. This isn't new. We've gone back and forth plenty of times but the tension I'm feeling coming from his side of the truck isn't something I've felt in awhile.

"Insanely, Winnie. I thought I was making that fairly obvious." There's finally a little humor in his voice when he says it and I am now full on belly laughing in the passenger seat. I'm wiping tears from my eyes when I ask my next question.

"Why in the world would you be jealous?" I force the words out. He's quiet for a minute. I look over at him when I feel the truck slowing. The expression on his face and the way he's looking at me makes heat curl low in my stomach. His answer stokes that flame.

"Because you're beautiful Winnie and it seems like everyone in my family got to touch you tonight except for me." His low voice sends goosebumps dancing across my limbs... limbs that now feel like jell-o.

"Why would you want to touch me?" I'm on the edge of a cliff right now. He let's out a sigh and looks out the windshield as he comes to a stop in front of my house. I'm not going to get an answer when I desperately need to know what he's thinking. He clears his throat and I take it as a sign I should get out but as I open the door Rhett grabs my arm.

"Can I come out with you for your birthday?" Not what I thought he was going to say but I nod.

"If you want to."

"I want to." He's smiling again and just the sight of it has my lips twitching, too.

"Okay. I guess I'll see you then." I go to get out again but he stops me again. I huff and look at him.

"Yes, Rhett?"

"What if I want to see you before?" I laugh.

"You can stop by the bakery. I'm always there. Oh, and in case you weren't aware. We're neighbors now, so I'm sure you'll see me so much you'll be sick of me." He shakes his head.

"Not possible. What are you doing the rest of the day?" His question catches me off guard.

"Uh, I'm not sure. I need to catch up on some laundry and I have a really good book I'm reading."

"Bring the book."

"Bring the book? To? Where?" He's completely lost me.

"Go get your swimsuit on and something to hike in, I'll be back in 20."

"Hiking? I know I said I had been trying to get out more but—"

"It's just to the lake, one small hill." He can see the uncertainty. "Please." That does it.

"Fine. I'll see you in 20." His answering smile is one of my favorites, it's the one he uses when he gets something he really wants. I would do almost anything for that smile. Like go on a hike on my only day off this week.

RHETT

I'm smiling 20 minutes later as I walk next door to pick Winnie up for our date. She may not know that's what this is, but she will. She was a little hesitant in saying yes to a hike, but I'm just taking her on an easy three mile loop that goes by the lake. It's supposed to get pretty hot today, so I told her to bring a swimsuit in case we decide to swim. I've got my backpack loaded with sunscreen, bug spray, towels, water, and a small picnic. I wish I could have gotten a better selection but salami, cheese, crackers and some fruit will have to do. I shake my head, still floored that she accepted my invitation to go on a hike. Willingly.

She said that she's been trying to hike more but it's hard to believe when I've seen her on a trail. I wince at the memory. She managed to get poison ivy the last time Colt convinced her to come with us. That's not the easiest thing to do in Colorado, but she fell into a patch, wiped the hair out of her face and by the time we got home...her face...oh man, it was so swollen she could barely see. Mom and dad took her to Dr. Jones' office and she had to get a shot and slather her face in cream. She vowed that night that she would never go on a hike with us ever again. So, imagine my surprise when she agreed to go with me.

I walk up her steps and knock on her door. I hear a thump and then she opens the door for me. She's rubbing her elbow.

"You okay?"

"Hello to you, too." She smiles.

"Hi," I say grinning as I lean on the doorframe. "Are you okay?" I point at her elbow.

"Oh...yeah. I'm fine, just clipped my elbow coming around the corner to get the door."

"Eager to see me then?" She blushes.

"Oh, get over yourself will you?" I give myself a minute then to take in her appearance. Her hair is tied back on the back of her neck with little pieces escaping and curling at her face, freckles are on full display. She's got on an orange tank top and tight little black shorts There's a small sliver of skin showing across her waist and my eyes bug out of my head when I see the hint of black ink on the right side of her stomach.

"What do we have here?" I motion to her stomach and she follows the gesture.

"Oh, well that would be a tattoo." She informs me.

"What is it? When did you get it? Can I see it?" She dissolves into a fit a giggles.

"Now who's eager?"

"I'm not ashamed to admit it. I really want to see your tattoo right this minute. I have no chill." She's still giggling as she inches the tank top up and pulls the band of her shorts down just enough for me to see.

"It's a rosemary sprig." I run my eyes over the design, from the outside of her ribcage, curving across her belly and back down towards her hip.

"When did you get this?"

"Um, I got it on my 24th birthday. It symbolizes remembrance." She swallows. "I wanted to have something physical to remember my parents." She puts on such a tough exterior, but I know she struggles with losing them at such a young age.

"That's really special, Winnie. It's beautiful."

"Thank you. I don't always remember them that clearly but I thought this would be a way to keep them with me." She reaches next to the door and grabs a book and a little bag that she slings over her chest. It's just big enough to slip the book in. She grabs a chapstick and puts a worn green plaid flannel on. She's not even trying and she looks so adorable I can hardly stand it.

"Have you read it?" I look at her confused.

"What?" She taps her little bag.

"The book."

"Oh um, no. I haven't read it. What's it about?"

"Well, if you haven't read it. It's kind of hard to explain."

"I better read it then." Her mouth pops open a little. "As good at distracting me as you have proven to be—I do have a date planned."

"A date? I think you mean a *hike*." She pulls on her boots over her tall socks and laces them up. "Well let's go be one with nature then." I grin at her fake enthusiasm.

"Let's go, honeybee."

The ride to the trailhead is only 30 minutes. I've looked over at Winnie as much as possible in that time. Having missed so much time with her over the years I don't want to waste anymore. I have the windows rolled down and the sunroof open in the truck. I'm distracted by Winnie's hair blowing around in the wind, despite having tried to contain it in a bun. I let out a laugh and she looks over at the sound. I can see myself reflected in her sunglasses and I look happy. Really damn happy. I feel that way, too. For the first time in a really long time. I loved hockey and I loved playing professionally but as great as it was it never made me this happy. She laughs with me as we pull into the parking lot.

It's around 2 by the time we get started and the sun is as brutal as always. Once we get to the tree line we'll have a little shade for a while. I notice Winnie's shoulders already getting pink.

"Did you put on sunscreen?" I take my pack off and search for the SPF 50 I picked up just for her while she sits on a rock.

"I did actually but I probably missed some spots."

"I came prepared."

"You were a boy scout." I chuckle at that.

"I was but how would you know? I was done with that before you moved."

"Ohhh Rhett... I have seen pictures. Many pictures. So many badges. It's honestly a wonder you had time for hockey with all the badge collecting you were doing." I sit behind her on the rock and rub some of the sunscreen onto her shoulders and down her arms. My tone turns serious.

"Are you making fun of baby Rhett?" A surprise laugh sputters out of her. That's my favorite laugh of hers, but only second to the one she does when she's laughing at something she said herself. I feel like I could move the mountain we're sitting on when I'm the reason she's laughing like that.

"Oh, no. Never. I'm just telling you how impressive all those badges were." She snickers.

"I hope that's the truth." I warn as I put my pack back on.

"Well...I may have been teasing a little bit." She admits and I swat her behind.

"You did not just do that." Her tone sounds threatening but she's

"I did. Get a move on, Parker. We're burning daylight and as a former boy scout I can tell you we don't want to be out here after dark tonight." She starts giggling but continues on the trail.

"So how is it being Coach Holloway?" Winnie breaks our comfortable silence as we reach the trees.

"Honestly? It's great. I wasn't sure how I would feel not being out in the action anymore, but watching those boys work hard and succeed, it's pretty awesome."

"I can't wait for your first game. You're going to be the best coach. You've always been a leader."

"You never listened to me."

"I wouldn't say I *never* listened to you. You and Colt were just always so bossy because you were older than me and I didn't think that was a good enough reason to listen to you." I laugh loudly at that.

"You have always done exactly what you wanted to do. That's something I've always admired about you."

"Thanks. It's funny though because I've always thought the same of you."

"I'm not too unaware to say that I haven't done what I've wanted to do in my life, but I would have done whatever you wanted, pretty much at any time over the course of knowing you." I can see her blush from here.

"That's not true, Rhett," she says quietly.

"It is. All you had to do was ask." She turns her torso to look at me behind her.

"Can I ask you something now?" Her tone is low.

"Anything," I say as earnestly as I can. She leans closer and slides her sunglasses up on her head to look me in the eyes. Heat licks up my spine.

"How much farther to the lake?" she whispers softly and then throws her head back laughing at herself. Yes, that is my favorite laugh.

"You are such a brat!" I shoulder her stomach and lift her up onto mine as I stand and smack her behind once more. She's giggling and swatting at me.

"What? It's hot and I just wanted to know!" I carry her the last few feet till we come to the end of the shade and into the clearing with the lake nestled into the base of the mountains.

"Here." I state, setting her down. She looks around us, taking in the view.

"It's really beautiful here."

"I love this spot. It's not as well known to the tourists but fairly easy to get to."

"That's my favorite part." I smirk.

"Are you hungry?"

"I could go for a snack. What did you bring us?"

"Don't get too excited, this is just what I could find at the grocery store today in five minutes." She smiles and leans down to where I'm pulling out a blanket.

"This is great, Rhett—and very sweet." She tacks the last thing on like she's suspicious of it.

"You sound surprised."

"You have definitely surprised me. This is really sweet and I'm glad I came, even though I am starting to sweat and may

have to get in the water to cool off before I can enjoy all this."
She motions to the small snack pile and I smile.

"I'm so glad you said something. I'm burning up." I stand
and slip my shirt off. She leans back onto her elbows and
openly stares.

"You've got a little drool right there..." I use my thumb to
wipe the corner of my mouth and laugh.

"I'm just enjoying the view, Holloway."

"I am...okay with that, but I don't want to swim alone so, up
you go." I grab her hands and pull her up. She unzips her small
backpack and pulls out a green bikini top. It's my turn to tease
her. I cross my arms over my chest, looking at her and smile.

"Turn around..." She twirls her pointer finger in the air and
I chuckle but do as she says. I look out over the lake and the
mountains that I love so much. I have missed home. I didn't
hate Washington, but I hated being in the city so often. It's
always loud and noisy. It's peaceful here. It's peaceful being
with Winnie. I didn't realize how calming being with her can
be. She would argue that her anxious energy isn't calming but
having her depend on me helps me feel grounded. I feel her
light touch on my back, tracing one of my tattoos.

"Do all of these have significant meaning or did you just
like them?"

"I'd say it's a 50/50 mix. Some of them were more thought
out than others."

"And this one...?" She glides her finger over my forearm
where I have a water scene.

"That one was thought out, done in three sessions. It's clear
creek."

"I can see that now."

"It's one of my favorite places to be."

"I remember this one. The hockey sticks are pretty self explanatory." I can hear the smirk in her voice and turn to look at her and maybe it was better to not be looking at her while she's touching me if I want to keep the slow pace that I'm trying to go at. Winnie Parker is a dream. She's taken her hair out of its bun and it's hanging over her shoulders in wild curls. There's a spark in her eyes, knowing that she's driving me crazy. I feel like I'm getting hit with wave after wave, again and again, with how impossibly beautiful she is. I swallow.

"I got that one the day I turned 18."

"The same day Colt got his raft." She chuckles. "Cute."

"Yeah, you think that's cute? You should see the best friend necklaces we got." She laughs and I pick her up again and run towards the lake as she squeals and giggles. I run us into the cold water and then dive under, pulling her along with me. When I break the surface I hear her before I see her.

"Oh my gahh...it's freezing!" I see she's treading water a few feet from me and swim closer. I touch my feet to the bottom of the lake and stand next to her.

"Can you stand?" I nod and she grabs onto my arm. "Good, I need a break." I snort.

"You've been treading water for less than 15 seconds."

"That long?" I pull her around me and hook my arm under her legs to hold her bridal style. She leans back and closes her eyes, using my arms as a chair. She likes this, we spent a lot of time like this that summer. I just look at her. The sun hitting every perfect inch of her. I swing her back and forth in the water and watch as her hair floats around her.

"This is nice." Her voice is soft.

"Yeah, it is." I survey her face. The dark brows, upturned nose and the freckles that dot her skin like tiny constellations that I want to take a pen to and connect. That may sound like a serial killer move, but I don't care. She has her head laid back so I look down the column of her neck to her collar bones and shoulders where more freckles appear. The tattoo on the right side of her stomach and...do I see another tattoo...?

"What do we have here?"

"Hmm...?" She sounds so relaxed. I see a fern frond on her left hip tapering off onto her thigh.

"When did you get that?"

"Get what?" She opens her eyes and her eyes in the sun look like pools of honey that I want to swim in.

"The fern tattoo."

"Oh, I got that one a couple years ago. It was a cover up job." I laugh and she slips out of my arms to swim to more shallow water.

"A cover up? What did you get? I have to know." She smiles.

"Wouldn't you like to know? It was just a dumb spur of the moment decision." She keeps walking and when her back is finally exposed to me I see more ink.

"More tattoos?" There's a jaguar on the lower part of her left shoulder blade and a plant leaf on the opposite rib cage. "Winslow Parker, you rebel." She laughs at that.

"Look who's talking? You're covered."

"Yeah but I'm not masquerading as the innocent town baker." Her laughter grows.

"I am the innocent town baker." She deadpans.

"So she says...now back to the mystery tattoo that was so bad you had to cover it."

"I thought you were acceptably distracted."

"As distracting as you are, I've got to know."

"Hmm..." She taps her chin. "If you can guess it, I'll tell you."

"You're on." I follow her out of the lake, entranced.

We spend the rest of the afternoon laying on our blanket, snacking, talking and laughing. She reads her book and I'm happy to just be beside her, catching glimpses of her face, knowing when she likes a page. When it's time to make the hike back to the car I take every opportunity to help her down the mountain. Not only because I can't stop touching her but also because I'm worried she may trip and a visit to the emergency room would kind of put a damper on the amazing day we've had. And it has been an amazing day. I don't know what's going on in Winnie's head, sometimes it's a mystery but I know I can't stop smiling even after I drop her off at her house and am getting into bed, wishing I could be laying down next to her.

WINNIE

A few days have passed since our day at the lake. During that time, I've thought of little else. I've been back and forth on trying to have a casual thing with Rhett and I don't see how I don't fall for him and get my heart broken. He's been in and out of his house a lot. It's not that I'm keeping track of him. It's just hard not to when he lives right next door. I'm going to try and take my mind off of it though. Tonight I'm having Mare over for a wine night and trash tv. She's been working crazy hours at the hospital and I can tell there's more tension with another doctor, maybe I'll be able to get her to spill tonight.

It's beautiful out today. A little cooler than the last few. The season is starting to change and I can't wait for it. I brought home some things from the bakery to snack on tonight and I'm also making chicken fettuccine for dinner, because that's Mare's favorite dish and we like to carb load while watching other people derail their lives. I'm already in my most comfy pajamas when I hear her come in.

"Honey! I'm home!" she calls and I grin.

"In the kitchen! Right where I should be, sweetheart!" I reply and we both laugh.

"Is that amazing smell what I think it is?"

"It is," I confirm. "Because I'm the best friend anyone could ask for."

"You are the best friend anyone could ask for! I brought the wine. Should I open it now or?" I give the side eye. "Yep, opening now." She opens the two drawers she seems to always open before she gets to the one with the wine key. "So, how's it going with the new neighbor?" I filled her in on the night I gave Rhett a very accidental strip tease in my kitchen through a string of frantic voice messages.

"Um...fine I guess. I haven't seen much of him since Sunday."

"What was he doing Sunday?"

"We—went hiking...?" I focus on the sauce on the stove but I see her turn to face me.

"Hiking." She says the word like she's testing it. "You went hiking? Together?"

"Yeah. I went to his family's lunch, Mary invited me and then he asked me to go. I wasn't going to but he said I could bring my book and well...I've definitely had worse days." When I chance a look at her, she's shaking. "Mare?" I hear a snort. "What is so funny?"

"Winnie." She gasps out between the fit of laughter she's succumbed to.

"What?" I'm smiling now, too, because it feels weird not to join in at this point.

"He wasn't even here three days and you went *hiking* with him?" I laugh a little at that.

"Four days."

"Huh?"

"He was here for four days," I say with an eye roll and she loses it. "It's not that funny, Mare." She sobers a bit.

"I know, I know. It's just you told me after you went to see him at the hospital that you were done pining. You were going to move on. Then he comes back to town for all of five minutes and you've spent an afternoon with him?"

"When you say it like that I sound incredibly pathetic."

"No, Winnie. Not at all. You're just not really over him." I sigh.

"No I'm not. I don't know if I ever will be. Sunday was just proof of that."

"Oh, honey. So, what's the hold up?" I look at her.

"Don't look at me like that. You know what the hold up is."

"Why won't you believe what's so absurdly true, Win?" I let a long breath out.

"And what's that, Marigold?"

"You get to have a great love."

"I don't want to have a great love. A great love just means greater the heartbreak."

"Why are you so convinced you'll get your heart broken? What if it lasts?"

"It won't. Not for me. I'm difficult. I'm a lot."

"The right person wouldn't feel that way, Winnie. You haven't given him a chance to prove you wrong."

"It's too much of a risk." I spoon the pasta onto our plates and walk to the table where she sits with our wine. "Oh I almost forgot the garlic bread." I remove it from the oven and transfer it into a bowl. "So, how's it going at the hospital? Are you still having it out with the doctor from the radiology lab the other day?" Asking her about work is my attempt to deflect. I don't want to talk about this any more. I just want to have a fun night with Mare and let my issues fall to the side. I smile when it works and she launches into a story about stolen fridge yogurt and—

"—and he had the audacity to tell me if I *labeled my container more clearly* then he would have known it was mine, but like he obviously knew it wasn't his!" She holds her wine glass in the air, moving it around while she talks and I'm waiting for it to slosh over the side as I laugh.

"Let me guess. You didn't take that well?" She flashes me a sassy grin.

"It's like you know me or something." She places her hand over her chest when she says this and I grin.

"So, what did you do?" She laughs.

"Nothing." She takes a sip of her drink then tilts her head and adds. "—yet." Laughter bursts out of me. Marigold is the life of the party to my wallflower tendencies. She's a head turner in every sense of the word. She's a lot like Colt in that way. That's probably why they butt heads so often. I've played referee to countless matches between them over the years and it doesn't seem to be slowing down.

"I thought about *not clearly labeling* a laxative brownie. *Not clearly labeling* expired cream that he uses for his coffee. I'm not sure which direction to take this."

"I'm sure you'll come up with something good."

"I always do." She winks. I take our plates to the kitchen and rinse them before putting them in the dishwasher. I listen to more of Mare's ideas on how to get back at Dr. Steals Your Food. I cackle when she introduces that nickname to the conversation. After cleaning up I make a plate of snacks and she grabs the wine so we can move into the living room. We have at least three episodes of The Bachelor to catch up on. I'm thrilled! Nights like this are such a great reset for me.

When all the roses have been handed out and the snacks are gone I look over and see my best friend sleeping soundly. Her long shifts are catching up to her. I cover her with a blanket and take our dishes to the sink. After condensing all the food and cleaning up I remember tomorrow is trash day. I gather all the trash from the rest of the house to take it out to the curb. I open the door in the kitchen that leads to my side yard and throw the bag into the bin. A thud startles me. My hand flies to my throat as I snap my head up. I look over to see my neighbor taking his trash out as well. I relax and let out my breath.

"You scared me, Rhett." He smiles and starts walking to the fence that separates our yards.

"Sorry about that." I walk towards him.

"I guess it's not your fault, I just haven't had a neighbor in awhile."

"Butterfly?"

"What? Butterfly?"

"Your tattoo coverup. Butterfly?" I smile.

"Nope. Not even close."

"I'll figure it out eventually." He's so cocky sometimes, I swear. "How was your night, honeybee?" He's called me honeybee since we were kids, telling me once that it's because I'm sweet like honey until I'm cornered but then I sting like a bee.

"It was good. Mare's asleep inside. We had a wine and trash tv night." He puts his hands on the black metal fence and leans onto them, closer to me. He's in a white tee and gray sweatpants with his feet bare. I cross my arms over my chest, remembering I'm in my pajamas.

"What show was it tonight?" he asks, his genuine curiosity is evident. I grin.

"The Bachelor." He grins back.

"Well go on then. Give me the highlights." I chuckle.

"Do you really want them? I always felt like it may have driven you crazy to listen to me recap everything." Rhett had always humored me and let me go on about my shows and books.

"If I'm being honest I've really missed hearing your recaps, I've missed hearing you in general." My chest warms and my heartbeat picks up. I tuck my hair behind my ear, trying to calm myself.

"Then you're in for a treat because I just watched three episodes." He smiles wide.

"I've got all night." Rhett's always made me feel important, like a priority. He wasn't always telling me with words, but he was constantly showing me with his actions. I have never doubted that when Rhett was with me, he wanted to be.

We spent hours outside, me recapping not only the last few hours of tv I watched but the years worth of books and shows that I never got a chance to tell him about. He gasped and looked shocked at all the right times, clapped for my monologues, and laughed with me when I remembered something especially ridiculous. When we said goodnight, I found myself wanting to stay with him. So now as I'm climbing into bed, smiling like an idiot, I'm hit again with how easy it would be to let myself fall in love with Rhett Holloway.

RHETT

I'm meeting my team at the rink today for our first practice and I'm a little nervous but mostly excited. I also have dinner for Winnie's birthday tonight. I've been reliving our moonlight catchup in the backyard on repeat the last few days. I need to have a conversation with her. Whatever we had years ago is still there and I want to try again. Now that we're older I'm wishing I could take her out alone tonight but we'll be going with Marigold and my brother, too.

I roll my eyes because I don't know if Alder's coming to get a rise out of me or if he and Winnie have gotten close over the years. When I asked him Thursday while we were biking, he wouldn't give me a straight answer. My brothers really know how to get under my skin.

I walk into the rink and it feels like home. I'm an hour early because I wanted to warm up a little before all the boys got here. My knee still gets really sore and I know it will be tight today after not skating for a few months. It was killing me after a couple hours of biking. I drop my bag in my office and grab my skates and stick. Being back on the ice feels like I never left. I do a couple line drills and laps until I'm feeling good. Then I set up some cones and work through a couple drills I want the team to do today. I want to see who stands out and who may need a little help. I'm starting to sweat a little when I hear the side entrance door shut and I look up to see a group forming.

I skate over to them and stop just at the wall.

"Hey guys. Why don't you all get laced up and meet me back here on the ice?" There's a lot of head bobbing and a couple 'Yes, Sir's'. That's gonna take some getting used to. I shake my head and smile to myself as I skate back to center ice. I'm warmed up and ready to see what this team has got.

I have them run through a handful of drills and I'm pleasantly surprised with the talent. There's a few that are head and shoulders above the rest, but for the most part there's a quality group of boys here. After drills I have them scrimmage to see how they think in a game situation. There's definitely some work to be done but we may have a shot at a winning season. I'm impressed and I'm genuinely excited about coaching this team.

To be honest I wasn't sure how I would feel from the sidelines and not being in the action. I show a couple of the boys some techniques to help with handling the puck and a better hold on their stick. My goalies are fairly solid but I have them take turns in the net blocking shots from everyone else for the last 20 minutes we're here. I blow my whistle and have them all circle up. They take a knee and stare at me. I feel a little pressure now having them look to me for words of encouragement and wisdom.

"You all looked good out there today. I can tell you've been putting in the work and our next season is going to show it, too."

"Woop!" "That's right!" "Let's go!" they all yell.

"I'm excited to keep seeing that hard work over these next few weeks. I know the season hasn't quite started yet but I've put together a weekly training and practice schedule along with some community events that I expect to see you all at." No groaning or complaining at that. They all look ready. I'm feeling pretty lucky that this is my team. Pride swells in my chest.

"Grab your schedule on your way out and everyone stay out of trouble." I see a couple of them exchange looks and that lets me know who I may have to keep my eye on. I change into my sneakers and by the time I have my duffle and I'm in the parking lot my knee is aching and I'm starting to limp a little. I told dad I would help him at the ranch this afternoon before getting ready to go out for Winnie's birthday so I pop a couple ibuprofen and drive out there.

He's out by the barn when I pull up, so I park as close as I can, not wanting to have to push my knee any farther today.

"Hey, son! How'd practice with the team go?"

"Good. Really good actually. They're a solid group. I'm excited to get to work with them and see how far I can push them. They've got talent and most of them seem to have the drive."

"Ah, a lot like you then?" He smiles and claps my back. "I'm really proud of you Rhett. I had worried you may not settle back in so easy after your injury but you really seem to be doing well."

"It's always been part of the dream to be back here, you know that. My injury just fast tracked that part."

"You're a good man, Rhett." He starts toward the four

wheelers that he already has loaded with tools to mend some fence. I follow and turn his words over as I do.

"I don't know about all that." At least we won't be riding horses, they sold all of them years ago but dad still has about 300 head of cattle out here.

"Why would you say that? You're a great son, brother, friend, soon to be coach. What's got you thinking less of yourself?" I contemplate lying but know he can spot BS from any of us kids a mile away. I blow a raspberry and lean against the ATV.

"That bad huh?" He chuckles and it helps to lighten the mood a little.

"I'm not sure if it's bad or not really. It doesn't feel that way but I'm not sure if everyone involved would feel that way." He nods, thoughtfully.

"Whatever it is, I'm sure you can work through it."

"I'm into Winnie." His booming laugh startles me. "Why is that funny?" That makes him laugh harder. What is going on with him? He's acting like I just told him the punch line from one of his joke books.

"I'm sorry son—it's just, I didn't realize you thought that was a secret." He's wiping his eyes with his handkerchief as his chuckles slow.

"What are you talking about? I've never once said anything about her or so much as held her hand in front of anyone."

"Oh, I know. You may have never spoken the words but I've seen the way you've looked at her since you were both teenagers. I've seen the way she's looked at you, too." I'm surprised by him knowing how long I've had a thing for Winnie. "But why does having feelings for that gem of a woman mean you aren't a good man? I'd say it makes you a good man with better sense."

"Because Colt is my best friend and even though he's never come out and said it, he's hinted that she's off limits." Dad scratches his head then and adjusts his ball cap.

"You're 33 years old Rhett. I would have thought someone telling you who to date was a thing of the past." Dad always knows how to cut to the heart of the matter.

"He's not just someone though and I get why he may not want me to date his sister. I don't exactly have a sparkling clean past with women."

"I think that's an excuse."

"It's just a fact."

"And you're supposed to be perfect? I think you're not giving anyone else in this equation a chance to decide for themselves." I thought about that. "...and maybe if you let them make up their own minds, the way they feel might surprise you." He gets on his own ATV and starts it up so I do the same. Tom Holloway is a wise man. He's given me advice my whole life and not once had it lead me down a road that wasn't the right one. Would Colt understand if I told him I wanted to be with his sister? Would he believe me if I said I wouldn't hurt her? I ask myself these questions and more as I help dad mend fence the rest of the afternoon.

I'm beat and in need of a shower when I get back to my house. My knee is starting to throb again and I take two more ibuprofen. I need to ice it for as long as possible. I know if I don't I'll regret it later, so I go downstairs and get my ice pack from the freezer.

I take the fastest shower I've ever taken, throw on some shorts and shirt, then sit on the small couch I have in my bedroom to ice my knee for 20 minutes. I'm supposed to meet Winnie, Alder, and Mare in 45 minutes, so that gives me plenty of time. I lay my head on the back of the couch and let the ice go to work.

My lap is covered in long dark hair that smells like sugar and vanilla. I can hear giggling. Winnie's giggling. One of my hands is tangled in her dark hair and the other is on her side lightly squeezing. She turns to look up at me and her warm whiskey eyes are full of laughter. Her grin is so adorable that the only thing I want to do is kiss that mouth. Her pink lips are pulled up at the corners and she raises a brow at me. I lean in and just as I touch my lips to hers—

I'm startled awake by my phone vibrating. I lift my head and grab at the back of my neck, why is it so stiff? Then I look around my now dark room. Wait, why is it so dark? I grab for my phone and check the time. It's 8:15. Also, a text from Winnie. No, no, no. I was supposed to have already been at dinner for her birthday. I have three missed calls from Alder so I tap his name, hoping they're still out.

"Where are you?" Is his answer, it's loud in the background.

"I fell asleep icing my knee, I'm getting dressed now. Are you still at dinner?" He scoffs.

"No, we're at AJ's and if you want to stand a chance I would get over here."

"What are you talking about?"

"You know what I'm talking about and you're not the only guy in town tonight that also feels that way." He chuckles.

"What the hell does that mean?" I growl into the phone, already having a decent idea.

"It means, you idiot, that Winnie is hot and more than one

man has noticed that tonight and bought her a birthday drink."
Shit. I don't like the sound of that.

"I'm on my way." I end the call and am putting on my shoes
when there's a knock. Who could that be? I race down the
stairs and open my door to see Colt standing on my porch.

"Hey, what are you doing here?"

"I'm heading to AJ's to see Winnie for her birthday and
thought I would stop by to see if you wanted to come with.
How was practice today?" Any other day this would be a
welcome invitation but tonight I was on a mission and it was to
let Winnie know how I felt. That would be hard to do with her
brother sitting next to me all night, but there wasn't anything I
could do about that now.

"Sounds good, I was heading there anyway." I grab my keys
and wallet and we take Colt's truck down the road and park on
the street in front of AJ's. I walk in and look around the
crowded space. I spot Winnie as soon as I pass the threshold,
she's giggling just like she was in my dream earlier only instead
of looking up at me, she's looking at someone else.

WINNIE

We walk into AJ's at 8pm...and by we I mean myself, Mare, and Alder. Rhett didn't show up for dinner and I haven't heard from him since we talked in my backyard a few nights ago. Knowing I was seeing him tonight I spent a little longer on my hair, doing my full curly girl routine. My thick brown almost black hair is long and hangs down my back. I applied some light makeup and took some care picking out my outfit. I decided on a sage green silky slip dress that I've never worn because it cuts lower in the front than I usually wear. I paired the dress with some nude sandals and called it good.

I'm trying to move on from the disappointment of not seeing Rhett. So I decide maybe I'll have a couple drinks and act like I'm a young 31 year old celebrating her birthday, it will be a good distraction from the constant thoughts of him. As hard as I've tried I'm still stuck on him. I look around the table, Marigold is a knockout. Long blonde hair, petite frame, she's a couple inches shorter than my 5'4", big blue eyes and a body she keeps in shape by doing all the outdoor sports you can imagine. She's my opposite in so many ways, but we work. I can't imagine my life without her in it.

"Win! My birthday girl! What are we drinking?! It's been too long since we've done this!"

"You were at my house drinking wine earlier this week."

"Like I said, too long." I laugh. "I'm thinking I'm gonna start with a beer. What about you guys?"

"A beer sounds good."

"I'll get us a pitcher," Alder says and walks over to the bar.

I take my jacket off, set it next to me and glance around. There are a few guys here tonight, some I don't recognize and a couple regulars. I check my phone for the millionth time tonight, hoping Rhett had checked in. He didn't, so I put it away for the night. Mare sees but doesn't comment. I mentioned to her this morning that Rhett was coming and now that he was a no show I looked a little pathetic. A very attractive clean cut man stops next to Mare.

"Fancy meeting you here." He smirks and she turns to glare at him.

"Grant. What are you doing out, don't you have an early shift tomorrow?" He answers yes and they start sniping at each other...ahh so this is Grant. The hot doctor from the radiology lap who steals *not clearly labeled* food.

"Grant, this is Winnie. Winnie, Grant."

"Nice to meet you, Winnie. I have heard so much about you."

"Yeah, I've heard a lot about you too." Mare nudges my foot under the table and shoots me a look. I shake Grant's outstretched hand and then he turns back to her.

"Back!" Alder shouts like I was timing him for a race and sets the beer pitcher and glasses down on our table.

"That was fast. The crowd is big tonight."

"The new bartender your uncle hired has a thing for me." I laugh.

"Oh yeah? And how did you discover this in the five minutes you've been here? Isn't tonight her first shift?"

"Win, sometimes you just know. And trust me, I know. She was giving me her most charming smile and she's been eyeing me since I walked in." That makes me laugh harder.

"I would not be surprised. You're a gorgeous man, Alder." He smiles and nods, agreeing with me. He's always been so good at accepting compliments, Mare is too. She's helped me get better at it over the course of our friendship.

"I think I'm going to go back over to the counter and see if I can get her number. I'll be back birthday girl." He kisses my cheek as he passes and I watch him saunter away. I shake my head at him. Grant says goodbye and moves back to his own table so Mare leans across the table and whispers.

"So, see anyone here tonight that looks like they'd show you a good time?"

"I'm not sure that's exactly what I'm looking for tonight but I see a couple guys I could be interested in."

"Yeah you do! Alright tell me who we've got our eye on." I love when she does this. She treats situations I'm not comfortable with like it's both of ours. As someone who used to have crippling anxiety it warms my heart.

"Okay, um, what about the guy over by the pool table?"

"The one with the 5 o'clock shadow or the blonde?" she asks.

"Not the blonde," I confirm.

"Yes, Win. That guy is hot. Like meet me in the bathroom hot." I blush but laugh.

"Marigold, I am not meeting someone in the bathroom." She just shrugs.

"Fine but I'll watch the door if you change your mind." she winks and I laugh hard before taking another long drink of my beer.

"Are we drinking tonight or *drinking* tonight?" I think about that for a couple seconds then decide what the hell? I don't have to be up early tomorrow since we're closed.

"We're *drinking!*"

"Woo! Hell yes we are!" she hollers and we raise our beers before downing them. "I'm getting us shots! Tequila!" I feel someone at my side and look over. It's the guy from the pool table.

"Tequila shots? Are we celebrating or commiserating?" His blue eyes twinkle and he has a cute grin on his face.

"Celebrating! It's her birthday!"

"No kidding, Happy Birthday! Do you mind if I join you?" He gestures to the empty stool and I look at Mare who is smiling and nodding.

"Sure, but only if you take a shot with us." I try for flirty...I think it comes out more stern than I wanted but he smiles widely at me.

"Count me in. I'm Nathan." He holds out a hand and I reciprocate.

"Great, I'm Winslow, but you can call me Winnie."

"I'll be right back with them," He says and makes his way toward the busy counter to order. I look at Mare who is already looking at me.

"Win, that was smooth. Who knew you had game?" I roll my eyes.

"Please, I have no game."

"I have to disagree with you there. You just got the hottie you had your eye on to buy us shots in less than two sentences. I'm impressed." I shake my head as Nathan makes it back with the shots and limes on the rims.

"Alright here we go."

"Three, two, one, go!" We all take our shots and grab for a lime wedge.

"I don't know why I ever think tequila shots are a good idea." I say as I pour myself another beer. "So Nathan, where are you from?"

"I'm actually from the Denver area, just here for the weekend, passing back through. We went rafting here last week before heading out to Rattlesnake Arches and our guide recommended this place."

"Oh yeah? Was your guide Colt Parker?" He looks surprised by my guess.

"Uh yeah, how did you know that?" I smile.

"Colt is my brother and the best rafting guide in Colorado." he laughs.

"Small world. Do you raft as well?" Mare can't stop her snort as she tries to hide her laugh in her beer.

"Uh no, actually. I'm not as big into outdoor sports as my brother. I'm not what you would consider athletic." I cringe... not really how I want to describe myself to a guy I'm trying to impress, but he catches me off guard when he laughs.

"You're adorable. So, what do you enjoy doing if not outdoor sports?" I blush at his compliment and am thankful for his interest.

"I bake. I actually own the bakery in town."

"You own it? That's amazing!" And it sounds like he really thinks that.

"Thank you, I've only been open a few months but it's going well."

"It's going fantastic," Mare interjects.

"So, what's your favorite thing to bake?"

"Ohh, that's a hard one..." I think about it. "I think my favorite thing to bake is chocolate croissants."

"You're kidding...those are my favorite to eat."

"Really?" I eye him skeptically.

"Honestly. You could have said anything and I would have said it was my favorite. I just want to keep talking to you." I blush.

"Well you don't have to fabricate favorite pastries. I'm enjoying talking to you, too." He smiles wide at that and I decide that maybe I could move on with someone like Nathan. He's handsome, charming, funny and maybe the most important quality is that he seems interested in me.

"So, how long have—" he's interrupted by my brothers booming voice.

"Win! Goldie!" Great. I turn and see him waving a beer pitcher in the air, somehow not spilling it everywhere, and coming our way...and then I see who's trailing him. *Even better.* I'm trying to forget about my embarrassing fixation with Rhett and that even when it shouldn't have, it hurt when he didn't show up for dinner. I need to let hope die. But he's walking towards me, looking so good, to be fair he always looks like that. He sees me and then he sees Nathan and I swear he looks annoyed. *Winnie...*I inwardly groan at myself.

"Hello, brother," I say in greeting as he sets the beer down.

"Happy Birthday, Winnie!" He wraps me in a hug.

"I hope that beer is for us," Mare chirps.

"It's for the birthday girl, but maybe stop being so bossy, Goldie."

"I'm not being bossy, Colt. It was only a question. You're always so defensive," She says innocently.

"I'm not being defensive." They're in a staredown now.

"Rhett." I nod at him then look away. I'm not sure if I should be but I'm mad at him. He basically admitted that he wanted to touch me the other day and then blew off my birthday dinner that he asked to come to. Mixed signals weren't something I handled well. They made me anxious. I liked to know the plan. I needed to know where things stood.

"Winnie. Happy Birthday."

"Thanks," I say without looking his way again and focus on Nathan. Colt grabs a stool from another high top and they crowd around our table. Colt squeezes next to Mare, so that puts Rhett right next to me. It wouldn't be so bad except his thigh is touching mine and his shoulder is brushing against me every time he moves.

"Hey, Nathan right? You were in my boat last week!"

"Yep, good memory. I decided to take your suggestion for a place to get a drink...imagine my surprise when it's your sister I find here." He throws me a wink and I know I must look like a tomato now. We all chuckle...except Rhett. He stays silent by my side. Nathan goes to stand and turns to me.

"It was really nice meeting you ladies but unfortunately I gotta head out. We've got a guided fly fishing outing planned for early in the morning. Winnie, I'm in town just a couple more days and I would really like to see you again. Would it be alright if I stopped by your bakery?" I'm disappointed that he's leaving already. That is not how I imagined my night with Nathan turning out, but hopefully I *will* see him again.

"Please do." I decide to wink at him this time and he grins.

"Looking forward to it." I grin back. He looks at Colt and Rhett. "Have a good night guys." Then he turns to go. I turn back to the table to see Mare and Colt looking stunned but smiling.

"What?" Mare laughs.

"Game! You absolutely have it, Win!" Colt laughs then too.

"Baby sister, it's a good thing I came in when I did. I think that poor guy was about to fall in love with you." I throw my head back at that.

"Oh, come on. I just met the guy. He was very sweet though."

"I don't know if the thoughts he was having were *sweet* but sure, he was sweet."

"Marigold!" I laugh loudly again and she and Colt join in, but when I glance to my right I see Rhett looking incredibly tense, jaw set in a hard line and eyes on the table. Not sure what his problem is but I refuse to ask. Tonight isn't about him, well it's kind of about not thinking about him...that's going great. Colt pours me a beer still chuckling.

"How was your week at the bakery, Win?"

"Good, we actually had someone in right at open one day." I smirk and look at Rhett again. He is now sitting up straight and looking at me with an anxious expression. Ookay...I'm assuming that look means *"Don't tell your brother it was me...?"* I give him a confused look and am about to ask why it matters but Colt starts talking again.

"No shit! That's awesome! I knew you'd be kicking ass right out of the gate. I'm so proud of you, Win."

"Oh, and congratulations on the house closing, Rhett!"

"Thank you."

"You closed on it so fast. You've been in town, what, a week?" Colt asks.

"I feel like you're underestimating how fast I can close a deal when I set my mind to it," he says it like he says most things, with a slight innuendo.

"Oh, I don't think anyone here is ever that surprised by how fast you close a deal..." I say. His grin drops a little.

"I've actually had my eye on this one since I was a kid and it just so happened to be for sale."

"Win lives right next door in the little white cottage directly behind there." Colt muses.

"Really?" he says and I know he already knows this. He spent all night talking to me in our adjoined backyards a couple nights ago. I go to say something about it but I see Mare look over my shoulder and turn just in time for a cute guy with light brown wavy hair to reach us and he's looking at me.

"Hey there. I saw you earlier but you were talking with someone else and I didn't want to interrupt. Do you think I could buy you a drink?" I blush and am flustered. I don't know what I'm going to say till I hear the words come out.

"Um, sure. That would be great." I smile and he holds out his hand.

"I'm Jared. Do you wanna come with me to the bar so we can get to know each other?" I look back at the table and Mare is nodding yes and waggling her eyebrows. I roll my eyes and Colt tips his head letting me know he's fine with it. I don't look at Rhett, I'm sure he disapproves. I just take Jared's hand and slide off the stool.

"I'm Winnie." He grins and leads me to the counter.

After spending about 12 minutes with Jared, it's obvious that we are not a match, but not wanting to face Rhett again just yet I stick it out for another 20. First of all, he doesn't eat sugar. He also keeps checking out every other woman in this place. I make an excuse about needing to get back to my friends. He doesn't put up a fight, obviously he isn't feeling it either. Before going back to the table I hit the bathroom.

I'm a tiny bit buzzed and looking at myself as I wash my hands. I sigh. Tonight wasn't a complete waste. In just under two hours I had some good conversations and possibly a follow up with a cute guy. I dry my hands and check myself in the mirror one more time, feeling confident, then push the door open. I make it two steps when I catch my sandal on the floor. The floor that is completely flat. We've been here before, many times. I brace myself for impact on the hard wooden surface but instead of the bruised hip and elbow I'm expecting to feel tomorrow, I feel strong hands grip my upper arms and then land face first into a very warm, very muscular chest.

"Oof! I'm so sorry! If you knew me, you would know that it's really not something I can help..." I'm babbling but trail off and stop talking when the smell of cedar and citrus hits me. I look up and see two green gemstone eyes looking back into my own. I forget how to breathe. *Rhett.* I swallow. Hard. He's looking at me with a level of intensity that is usually reserved for when he's on the ice. I take a shaky breath and try to regain composure. It's absolutely ridiculous to feel like this just because I'm close to him...why does it feel this good to be so close to him?

"Hey, Rhett. Just tripped. Sorry, I'll let you be." He doesn't release me though, instead his grip tightens slightly. He's still staring at me...glaring at me, really. "Everything okay, Rhett?" I see his jaw tick and he opens his mouth, then closes it. He sighs heavily and his hands slip down to my elbows. "Okay, well I'm gonna head back out there." I try to lighten the mood and move backward but it doesn't feel like it's working. He's stone faced and I'm starting to think maybe I should get a glass of water for my dry throat.

"Rhett? I think maybe I need to get some water, I'm feeling a little light headed. I don't drink very much and I'm remembering why right about now, I decided it would be okay since it's my birthday and all but yeah—I don't think I'll be doing this for awhile." He stops my rambling, thank goodness because I wasn't feeling capable but when he speaks I have a hard time understanding his words...

"Winnie, if I have to see you making eyes at another guy in this bar tonight, wishing to God it was me, I'm gonna lose my damn mind." His admission stuns me. I reach my right hand over to my left forearm and pinch myself. "Ow, shit!" So, he really did say that.

"What the hell, Winnie?! Why would you do that?" I stare blankly, trying and failing to absorb his words. He opens his mouth and I think maybe I'll get a longer explanation when I hear footsteps approaching and Rhett's hands fall away from my arms.

"Hey, there you guys are! Win, I settled our tab, are you ready to head out?" I nod and side step Rhett.

"Yeah, I'm ready to get home." My voice is off but luckily Mare seems to also be a bit buzzed and doesn't notice. Rhett clears his throat and I feel him move away.

"Can I stay at your place tonight? I'll just get my car in the morning."

"Of course, you know you don't even have to ask. Let's go."

I try to stop myself but can't fight the pull so I look back to where Rhett was just standing, only he isn't standing there anymore. Had I imagined that...? That's more likely to me than him actually saying what he did. *Wishing to God it was me...* yes, surely my imagination has finally jumped off the deep end tonight, but I look at my forearm and see the red mark from pinching myself.

I say goodnight to Colt as we pass the table. He already has two girls sitting at the stools beside him. Not surprised by that— although I am a little surprised that Mare doesn't look in his direction, actively ignoring him. Honestly those two are always fighting about something.

We talk about the guys at the bar as we walk home arm in arm. Laughing at the guy that hit on Mare tonight and called her sweetheart. She hates being called sweetheart more than she hates being called boring. We make it home just after 10. Mare crawls in my bed after removing only her shoes but I have to do my nighttime routine and change into pajamas or I won't be able to sleep. I throw my hair up in a bun, wash my face and then crawl in beside her. She already has some bad TV on and we settle in.

I'm halfway to sleep when I hear a husky voice repeating words I thought may have been a drink induced hallucination... *"...I'm gonna lose my damn mind..."* I try not to get ahead of myself though. I was better off not knowing what he meant or reading too much into it all. I guess it's time to see how easy it was to avoid someone in a small town.

RHETT

What the hell is wrong with me? A question that's been on my mind for the last seven days. A question I do not have the answer to yet. *What was I thinking?* Is another one. That one is easier to answer. I wasn't. It was pure impulsive instinct to tell Winnie what was going on inside my head. As soon as I saw her in AJ's—sitting next to that guy, smiling at him, looking beautiful, she always looks so damn beautiful, I knew I wouldn't last all night. I thought I had a handle on myself after he left but oh no, three minutes later and another idiot was dragging her away— she wouldn't even look at me.

I thought I was going to snap, maybe I had. I saw her going towards the bathrooms and followed. I followed her and waited for her to come out...actually waited, like some creep stalking the object of his obsession—I had no idea what I was going to say to her. Maybe I would just try to play it off that I happened to be there, too. Just to be near her, apologize for missing dinner and explain what had happened.

That was all I had wanted to do, but when I saw her walking out of the bathroom, flushed and smiling and heart-breakingly adorable, something loosened in my chest. Then she literally fell into my arms, her hair tickling my chest as I caught her. She smelled like vanilla and baked goods. She felt like home and longing at the same time. Then she looked up at me with recognition sparking in those warm amber eyes— I was done for. I realized in that moment, something I had been struggling with since I was 19 years old and my best friend's little sister was supposed to be off limits for me.

I wanted Winnie Parker and I was going to have to take a risk to get her.

About the time I came to that realization, she all but disappeared. I went back to our table to find Colt with two women I didn't recognize. Alder was chatting up the bartender, but Winnie and Marigold were gone. That was a week ago. I decided the morning after her birthday that I was going to pursue Winnie and ask her if she felt at all what I did, if she didn't yet, then I would show her that I could be worth her time.

I stopped by the bakery twice but Anna always had an excuse for why she couldn't come out. She was out getting something, she was busy in the back, she was doing inventory, this morning she was supposedly sick—the excuses were endless and I was coming to the conclusion my patience wasn't. Not about this. It felt like I had been waiting half my life already. I don't think she has been staying at her house every night either. The lights have been off, except for the one on the porch. I called her twice, this afternoon alone I had sent two texts. I wanted—no I needed to talk to her. I needed to know if she thought she could take a risk with me. She could try to keep avoiding me, but it couldn't last. Not only because there were only so many places she could dodge me in Silverthorne but because I wouldn't give up on her. There was also the handy fact that I was her neighbor.

I know she doesn't let people in easily, what she didn't realize is that I would take anything she would give me. Whatever pieces of herself she felt me worthy of, I would greedily take them and it would be more than enough. It would be everything. Now if she would just give me the time of day I could tell her all this. I would also tell her that it doesn't matter how many times she wants to push me away, I've been pushed into the boards plenty of times in my hockey career. I can take a hit.

That thought had me smiling as I walked into the high school's ice rink. I had the team on a schedule and we started meeting twice a week to lift weights and scrimmaging to get into playing condition. When I told them this was the schedule I was prepared for some groaning and complaining but these boys seemed excited to be getting to work and putting in the hours. They're already out on the ice when I walk in. I drop some things off at my office and then start looking over the pre-season schedule and planning out some community outreach.

Mary Holloway was big on community while all us kids were growing up, we all volunteered and were present at most town events. These boys will be too. It will also keep them out of trouble—mostly. I can tell which ones I'm going to have my hands full with. I lace up my skates and get out onto the ice with them. My knee is getting stronger, but it still hurts after my morning run and I have to ice it after every practice.

Two hours later, I dismiss my team and gather my things. I've decided I'll be making a visit to Winnie's tonight. If she thinks she can hide from me I'll have to prove to her that I don't mind taking on the challenge.

WINNIE

I feel like I've been hit by a truck...and that's coming from someone who was actually hit by a truck once. It was just backing up in a parking lot and I should have been paying better attention but still, it knocked me over. This though, this felt like my bones had bruises and those bruises had bruises. I left work this morning because I could feel the beginnings of migraine coming on. I had already made most of the pastries for the day so I felt confident in leaving Anna to man the register and then close early. I barely made it home before it hit in full force. I changed into my most comfortable pajamas and lay on the couch in my living room with a cool wash cloth covering my eyes for the rest of the day.

When I finally checked the time it was 6:30pm and there was a thunderstorm rolling in. I called Mare and she told me she would come over if I needed her to. I don't like to ask anyone to take care of me. I get migraines once a month, sometimes more. I think it's caused by my anxiety and it's been creeping to a higher level lately. I have been instructed to take a pain reliever and call her if I get any worse. I don't think I could possibly feel worse. My eyes were watery and my face was flushed. My hair was in a bun on top of my head and I was sweaty...then cold...then sweaty and cold. Miserable. At least I had a valid excuse for avoiding Rhett now.

He had called and texted a few times and even came by the bakery. I knew it was only a matter of time before I ran into him but I just wasn't quite ready for the conversation that no doubt would end in Rhett wanting something I wasn't sure I was willing to give him and my heart still somehow ending up broken. No, putting it off as long as possible was for the best, not the best for my anxiety, but for my heart. It didn't matter how much time passed, I was still a moth to his flame. A moth that had pined for the flame for over 15 years even though the flame had shown interest in the moth, but the moth was afraid that the flame would get tired of it's emotional baggage and leave.

Yes, I was still that moth. I let out a groan from the physical pain I was feeling but also the emotional turmoil I kept putting myself in.

I peel myself off the couch and walk into the kitchen in search of the bottle of ExcedrinPM I know I have in the cupboard. Maybe I can just sleep this thing off and maybe I could sleep through the storm, too. Thunderstorms still make me anxious. Not near as bad as those first few years after my parents died, but it still gives me a bad feeling. They were driving home from date night, just like they did every week. Colt and I ordered pizza and watched a movie. Since he had turned 15 the winter before we stopped getting a sitter. It was just me and him there when mom's sister, Aunt Sarah, showed up and said we had to get to the hospital right away. It had been storming that night, too. I feel physically ill thinking about how much of a brat I had been.

I think I used to like storms, the thunder sounding in the distance and rain spattering on our roof. I think I used to like that, but I can't really remember. It's been too long since I found any of the things that accompany a storm comforting.

I think my medicine is starting to kick in because I'm starting to feel a little fuzzy. My mind wanders back to Rhett as it does most days...more so now that he's back in town and messing with my head. It was so much easier when he was away. It's really not fair. I'm going to have to watch him find a woman he wants to marry, move her into the big beautiful house he just bought, be a fantastic husband to her, have babies with her.

Oh, God...I'm going to have to move aren't I? But I love my house. There's still so much I want to fix about it but I love my little house. It's the first thing I've had that was just mine. Something physical to show for all my hard work over the years. I don't want to give it up but I'm not sure what else to do.

My head is pounding still. It feels like someone is knocking from inside my head. I can feel the vibrations. I hear knocking and then my name, I giggle at that. Now they're even calling my name. I think I can hear a doorbell. Wait, was that my doorbell?

"Winnie! Open up! I know you're in there and I really need to talk to you." Huh? I open my eyes and look around my living room. Knocking again.

"I can wait here all night if I have to but it's starting to rain so I'd rather come in!" Is that Rhett? Oh, jeeze...why is he here? I'm really not up for a heart to heart right now. I stand and get a head rush.

"Hold on, I'm coming. Please quit knocking." I sound as awful as I feel, I try to speak loud enough for him to hear me, but I can't force my voice any louder. I unlock the bolt and sliding chain and open the door and let out a whine. There standing on my porch in the rain, is Rhett Holloway looking like he belongs on the cover of a magazine, which he has been on the cover of plenty of magazines and hockey calendars. Just another inadequacy between us. One other being the walls I've built around my heart and his open borders.

"What are you doing here, Rhett?"

"Jeezes, Winnie. You look awful—well you're always beautiful but you look sick."

"Did you come here to charm my pants off? Because the insults are really working for me." That gets me an eye roll.

"When Anna told me you were sick this morning I thought it was another excuse. What's wrong?" So he had noticed...

"Headache," I say as blandly as possible.

"It seems like more than a headache, Winnie." He retorts. "Why didn't you tell me?" I give him a confused look.

"Why would I tell you?"

"Well for one, I've been calling and texting and was starting to think you must be ignoring me..." He gives me a very pointed look. "...but also because someone should be taking care of you."

"I'm fine, Rhett. I can take care of myself."

"It's not that I don't think you can, darlin'. I just don't want you to have to." *Darlin'.* Hearing him say that sparks a memory. Honeybee had been my nickname since I was 13, but *Darlin'*, he only started calling me that after he kissed me at the lake eight years ago.

"Why are you calling me that?" I snap and he sighs.

"Would you just let me in? It's raining and I want to make sure you're okay."

"Uhhhg...fine." I open the door all the way and steps into my home. He looks around and surveys my cramped space.

"I like it. It's very you."

"Messy and in need of some work?"

"I was going to say warm and beautiful." My face heats. "You've done a great job with renovations." I wasn't expecting that.

"Thank you. I still have a ways to go, but it's getting there."

"Why don't you go sit on the couch and I'll get you something to eat."

"You don't have to do that. I'm not that hungry."

"Fine. Let's just sit on the couch and I'll find us something to watch while you rest." He plops onto my couch and grabs the TV remote from the arm.

"You want to stay?"

"Yes, if that's alright."

"I guess so...but why do you want to stay?"

"Is it so hard to believe that I want to spend time with you?"

"No, I'm charming and incredibly funny—" He smiles at that. "—but right now my head feels like there's something inside of it, pulsing before it finally explodes." His brows pull together and he starts studying me.

"Winnie, you look exhausted—just come sit by me and rest for a bit." I am exhausted. I'm barely staying upright so I relent.

"Fine." I take the few steps until I'm standing in front of him and he pats the seat next to him and smiles.

"I won't bite Winnie...not unless you ask nicely." He throws me a wink and I snort at that, then wince at the painful action, but sit next to him. He immediately puts his arm around my shoulders and pulls me into him so I'm tucked into his side, head resting on his chest. I instantly relax into him.

"Dragonfly? Playboy Bunny? Angel wings?"

"What?"

"The cover up." Is all he says. I try not to laugh because the pain in my head is already too intense.

"Nope. None of those."

"I'll figure it out. Now, what should I watch?" I have been here before with him many times, Rhett is an amazing cuddler —I feel safe with him. That's kind of the problem.

"You can always watch a cooking show, or catch up on The Bachelor first hand." I smile knowing he's pretty caught up because of our conversation the other night.

"You can pick whatever you want, though. I have all the hockey channels."

"Why do you have all of those?" There's teasing in his tone. He knows why. Because I've watched every single one of his games. Even when I was heartbroken after having gone to see him that last time. I decide to tease him back.

"Maybe I have a thing for hockey players. Some of those guys are unbelievably hot, Rhett." I talk as quietly as I can. I want to talk to him, but the pounding in my head won't subside.

"Which guys?" I smile because he sounds jealous again.

"Oh there's the defensemen that plays for San Francisco... the center for Vancouver...oh and the goalie for Dallas...I have a list..."

"A list, huh? And how long is this thing?"

"Oh, last time I checked there was maybe 30, 35 names on it...? That's just a ballpark." He runs his hand over my arm in soothing circles, his fingers trailing up and down. He moves up to my neck and gently massages. I'm melting.

"Yeah? That many? And where am I on this list?" I know what he's doing.

"Who says you're on it, Holloway?" I barely get it out without moaning when the pressure he applies to either side of my neck increases.

"Ouch." He stops massaging me and grabs at his chest in mock pain. "You're telling me not only did I not make top 5 but I didn't even make the list at all?"

"I know it's a huge blow to that ego of yours, but no. I'm sorry. You are not on my fantasy hockey league roster..." He looks at me seriously then.

"I don't think I've ever been more disappointed to not make a team in my life." My laughter sputters out of me at that and I whimper.

"Uhg, don't make me laugh. It hurts and I know for a fact that's a lie."

"Sorry." He starts massaging my neck again. "And nope, this is it." I scoff.

"What about first round draft picks your freshmen year?" I open my eyes to look up at him and find him already looking at me. He is really playing this up for me. He genuinely looks like he's contemplating. I pinch his leg.

"Okay, that was a rough one. I'll admit."

"That's what I thought."

"...but..." Oh here we go. "Not making the cut on a list or team of yours that has the word 'fantasy' in the title is worse than not making any other team I can think of." I roll my eyes.

"Always the charmer." He chuckles beside me.

"Only for you, honeybee."

I clear my throat not wanting to give weight to his words any more. I've had enough of the flirting that can't go anywhere with him. I fake a yawn which turns into a real one and then go to stand up.

"Where do you think you're going? I'm getting ready to start Chopped," He says holding up the remote.

"I just need to get a glass of water." What I really need is some separation.

"I'll get it. You need to rest." He lays me back into the couch before getting up. I hear him in the kitchen opening cabinets, trying to find a glass, the sound of distant thunder is like a backtrack. I don't even realize I've shut my eyes until I feel an arm slip under my knees and another wrap around my back. I'm cold but feeling sticky. Uhhgg and my head is hurting again. I'm swaying and then floating before landing on a soft surface. Mmm...that's nice. A cool hand touches my forehead and I hear mumbling but my eyelids are simply too heavy to be bothered to open. I feel something else touch my forehead and then my name.

"Winnie, you need to take a drink of this water for me."

"Uhhggdonwanta..."

"I know you don't want to, darlin', but you need to."

"Uhhhggg..." I lean up, with a hand supporting the back of my neck and feel the cool hard rounded edge of a glass, I drink three gulps of water.

"Did you get enough?" I try to nod.

"Mhmm..." I'm gently lowered back to the pillow and covered with blankets. What a strange feeling this is. I don't remember the last time I was this taken care of or felt this safe especially with thunder rumbling the walls of my little cottage and rain pouring down. I don't want to be alone anymore. I want him to stay, but I won't ask. I want him, but I won't tell him that. I'm thinking about how lucky that fictitious wife of his is going to be and then how I really will have to move when that happens. I won't be able to handle it. Those are the medicine induced thoughts that pull me under and into a surprisingly dreamless sleep.

RHETT

My face is warm and my eyelids are turning red, so I know that the sun is up. My back is stiff and I feel a dull ache in my knee. I open my eyes and last night comes back in a rush. I slept on Winnie's couch last night after taking care of her. Her migraine had gotten worse after I put her to bed and I was worried, checking on her every hour or so when I woke up to her talking in her sleep. She finally settled down and quit mumbling about 3 this morning so I decided I could come out here for the rest of the night...or morning really. I wasn't going to stay in her room, but mixed in with all the nonsense about having to move, she had asked me to stay.

My heart had done a funny little flip at that. I don't think she realizes that she could ask anything of me and I would do it but this was a request I was far too happy to agree to. I lay beside her with her small hand warm in mine, and the other gripping my arm in her sleep. As much as I hated that she was so sick, I loved the feeling of holding her hand in mine. I look around and take in the room. It's like a little greenhouse in here. There's vines and potted plants everywhere. I guess I didn't notice them last night when I invited myself in. I sit up and and stretch my tight muscles that are in desperate need of movement.

When I got here last night I fully expected to tell her that I missed her, I wanted to spend time with her, ask her to stop avoiding me. I was going to ask her on a date. A real one. I wanted her, and I was going to make my move. Then she opened her door and it was obvious she was actually sick. Anna had told me she had left the bakery yesterday morning, but I really thought it was just another excuse. She looked so miserable. I wanted to hold her and take care of her. She was always worried about everyone else. When she had sank into me on the couch, it felt like I could sit on a couch with her beside me for the rest of my life. Why had I wasted so much time trying to stay away from this woman?

I start a pot of coffee and look inside Winnie's fridge. I would bet she didn't eat much yesterday and even though I'm not a chef by any stretch of the word, Mary Holloway made sure her boys wouldn't be helpless men, so I can make a decent breakfast. I find eggs, bacon, her waffle iron and some strawberries. I can work with this.

I pour waffle batter into the iron and get the bacon going then see a small watering can and mister on the counter by the sink. In between making waffles and flipping the bacon I walk around her place watering her plants. I like being in her space. She's done a great job with the renovations. The butcher block counter tops and the jade green back splash. The wooden floors have been refinished, too. I'm leaning against the island drinking coffee and admiring her charming home when I hear her soft voice.

"Hi."

I turn to look at her and am momentarily stunned. She's taken a shower and changed. Her hair is damp and making wet spots on her thin t-shirt. Her face is completely void of makeup and I can see the freckles that I have loved and pictured just like this many times. Her lips are set in a tiny shy smile and she's leaning against the doorway with one foot propped on her other calf.

"Morning, darlin'. Are you feeling better?" A blush that I love stains her cheeks.

"Good morning. I am. My head feels back to normal weight and size. Are you cooking?" She sounds confused.

"Yes. I thought you may be hungry. How are you feeling?"

"I'm good, much better than last night." She peers around me to the waffle iron on the counter and stovetop. "What are you making?"

"I hope you still like waffles. You used to help my mom make them for us on weekends." I flip two onto a new plate and top them with chopped strawberries then put a couple pieces of bacon beside them. I hold it out to her but notice she's staring at me, specifically my bare torso. I grin. She's looked at me like this more than once but having her look at me and see the heat in her eyes doesn't ever get old.

"Winnie? Do you still like waffles?" I stare at her and she has a sweet dreamy look on her face. My grin widens as she shakes her head a little.

"Oh uh, yeah, this looks great. Thanks." She's blushing and I can't help but tease her.

"My eyes are up here, Parker." She snaps her head up and meets my gaze, the pink spots on her facing deepening to a light red. I lift my eyebrows and hold out the plate again. She takes it and sits at the round dining table. She turns her attention to the bacon on her plate and takes a bite. I may not be a chef but I would cook for Winnie every morning if she would let me. Thinking about having mornings like this reminds me of why I came here last night. I'm thinking about how to bring it up when she clears her throat again.

"You know, you didn't have to stay the night, I would have been fine. I called Marc earlier in the day and was following doctors orders...but thank you for taking care of me. It was really sweet of you." She's frazzled this morning, I love listening to her ramble when she's nervous, it's adorable so I mess with her again.

"I didn't mind. It was a very eye opening night." I wink and she chokes a little, coughing.

"What do you mean eye opening?" I grab a glass from the cabinet I found them in last night and get the orange juice out of the fridge to pour her a glass before answering.

"You talked in your sleep, said some really interesting things..."

"No, I didn't! Did I?" She looks way more worried than I would have thought and that makes me incredibly curious. What could she possibly think she said? "What did you hear? I was in a lot of pain last night, so I doubt it was even coherent."

"Mmm ...I don't know, Winnie. Sounded like you'd been thinking about these things for awhile." I smirk and she loses it.

"Barrett Holloway, tell me what I said right now."

"Easy, Win." I'm chuckling at her stern approach. "Take a breath. You didn't say anything I didn't already know." Her eyes flash.

"...and that would be?..."

"You only said that you think I'm the hottest man you have ever laid eyes on, that you were hopelessly in love with me, I was actually at the top of your Fantasy Hockey Player list and something about wishing you could have my babies...I think there was more, let me think for a second." A towel hits me in the face and I laugh.

"That isn't funny, you idiot!" She's laughing too, but the relief is evident.

"Sure it was. As much as I would have enjoyed you saying those things... you didn't, but you did ask me to stay...and some other things that I couldn't make sense of, something about having to move...?" Her face is now tomato red. I have no idea why it would be, but I really want to know. "What are you hiding from me? What did you really think you said?"

"Nothing....like you said, nothing you didn't already know."

I sit in the chair next to her and put my hand on her forehead. "Your color looks better now, so that's a good sign." I want to slide my hand to her cheek. She's too beautiful for words.

"I'm fine now. I think the worst has passed. Thank you again for staying...and for breakfast, but you can get going if you have other things to do today."

"Are you kicking me out the morning after, Winnie? Is that how it is?"

"No! Not that...no. I...I'm not. We didn't...That's not even..." She takes a deep breath.

"You are so adorable when you're flustered, Winnie Parker." She winces a little but tries to hide it by looking away. Maybe I've read this whole thing wrong and I'm making her uncomfortable, but she doesn't look uncomfortable. She looks mad.

"What's wrong? What did I say?"

"Nothing. It's just that's the word you used when you told me you didn't want to see me a couple years ago." She stands and takes her plate to the kitchen counter. I'm not sure what she's talking about. I've called her adorable many times before, but I can't remember a time when I didn't want to see her. I'd give anything to understand what just happened. Anything to go back to a few minutes ago when we were laughing in her kitchen together.

"When did I say—"

"It's fine." She cuts me off and gives me her fake smile, but looks like she may be about to cry. What the hell did I say? "It's really fine, Rhett. Thank you for coming to check on me last night and staying to help me out. You're a good friend." *Friend.* That is not a strong enough word I want to use for her anymore and I'm about to tell her that but she continues before I can. "I'm sorry I asked you to stay." Her eyes are filled with unshed tears and it's killing me. "I should probably get ready and head to the bakery since I left early yesterday and I need to start getting things ready for a few special orders we have coming next week." She sniffs and moves to the entry so I have no choice but to follow her. I grab my shirt on the way and slip it over my head.

"Hang on for just a minute. I'm not sorry you asked me to stay. I wanted to be here and take care if you. What's got you so upset? Winnie, talk to me." She swipes at her beautiful face and I feel like I've been punched in the gut.

"God, I'm so embarrassed. It was a long time ago. I should be over it. I guess it just hurt because I wasn't over you then and you— well you were moving on all over the place." She trails off and I am confused...she opens the front door and I shut it again.

"Rhett. Please don't make this a thing. I'm fine. I think I'm just tired because I was sick last night."

"I'm not going to leave here with you like this." I move to pull her to me but she puts her hands up. "I'm sorry for whatever I said or did that's upset you. How can I fix this?"

"You don't have anything to be sorry for. It's my fault I'm upset. I should be passed this..."

"Passed what, darlin'? You've lost me."

"Enough with the darlin', Rhett. We left all that behind eight years ago and I don't even know why I'm upset. I'm not offering you anything." She's rambling but I'm pretty sure I'm following now and I need to let her know that she's got it all wrong.

"Do you know how I feel about you, Winnie?"

"Why are you making me say this, Rhett?" Tears are flowing freely now. She has no idea. No idea that I've been forcing myself to hold back. That I've had to fight every instinct in my body to grab her and kiss her so many times over the years I've lost count.

"I want to know what you think I feel about you."

"I'm a memory, Rhett. Maybe a good one, but just a memory."

"Is that really all you think I feel for you, Winnie? That you're just something from my past?"

"I know it is." *What?* That stops me.

"When? When did I ever say that to you?" I know that I didn't, because it would have been a lie and I've never lied to her.

"When I went to see you!" Her shouting stuns me. I don't think I've ever seen her this angry. She blows out a breath, trying to calm down... "...about two years ago after you got hurt at a game." I think back, wracking my brain trying to remember which game she's talking about. Two years ago...that was here in Colorado. I had gotten tossed into the boards and ended up with a dislocated shoulder, but she wasn't there. No one had been there because Hazel was being born, it had taken mom six hours to get there, insisting she needed to be there. "I...I went to the game. Alone. I was going to ask you to give us another chance, tell you that I had missed you." Her voice is low now, so quiet I'm straining to hear her. She had come? "You ended up at the hospital." She looks like she's in pain just talking about this, her lip is quivering and the sight is breaking me. "I didn't want to go in but I was worried about you." She swallows. "So I went in and just sat in the waiting room." I know how hard that must have been for her. Her anxiety around hospitals was still bad and she had been there alone. I cringe. Why wouldn't she tell me she was there?

"You were there? I didn't know. Why were you there? Why didn't you come see me? I would have made sure you stayed with me." She gives me an incredulous look.

"I tried to." Now she's angry again. "I texted you, remember?" No, she didn't.

"No, you didn't. I would remember that, Winnie."

"Yes. I did. I remember the exchange vividly."

"I did not get a message from you that night." She looks at me with rage now.

"That's enough, Rhett. Why are you being like this?" She huffs, indignantly and takes off for her bedroom. I'm afraid she's going to lock me out but when I reach the door she's walking towards me with her phone in her hand, scrolling.

"What are you doing, Winnie?" She stares at her phone and starts reciting lie after lie.

"Let me refresh your memory since I guess you've taken too many hits to head out on the ice. You said you didn't need me there, you already had someone to take care of you and as adorable as it was that I followed you around like a puppy, I really needed to move on. Then you finished with the big finale, 'We had fun, but that's all it was, Winnie. Sorry.'" She looks up at me then. "I still have the messages on my phone as embarrassing as that is."

"Let me see them."

"Are you serious?"

"As a heart attack. I didn't text you that night." She hands her phone to me and I'm not quite understanding until I reread the part about someone taking care of me.

Ah. *Lacey.* Lacey had been there with me. I wince. Lacey and I had a very brief, very superficial relationship. We weren't even together at that time but she had insisted on coming to see me at the hospital.

"I was so mortified, so I waited for your mom to get there and went home."

"Winnie. I didn't say those things."

"What? Would you stop? You know you sent them and I have the messages right there on my phone."

"It wasn't me though. That's what I'm trying to tell you. It was an ex of mine. She showed up at the hospital and tried to get back together with me. She asked to use my phone while she was there and I didn't think anything of it. I never got your message, Winnie. I would have..." She holds her hands up.

"You don't have to do that, Rhett. In fact I would really prefer you didn't. I'm a big girl and it was a long time ago and it's not your fault that I had some idea in my head and expected you to reciprocate."

"But I would have. I did." She opens her mouth but I keep going. "I wasn't over you, Winnie. I don't think I'll ever be over you."

"Please don't say things like that to me...It isn't fair. Not to either of us."

"It's the truth. I have wanted you for as long as I can remember and I don't want to hide that anymore." She looks shocked, but I keep going. "That's why I came here last night. I was going to ask you for a second chance, as a grown man and not a boy who wouldn't fight for you or too worried about what his friend would think, but then you were sick and I just wanted to take care of you and this isn't how I wanted to do this." I take a deep breath before continuing. "I wanted to sweep you off your feet. Show you that I can be someone worthy."

"Worthy? Of what? What are you saying exactly?"

"I'm saying that I want you, Winnie." She doesn't look convinced. "Come here," I say as softly as I can.

"Why?" I answer by reaching over and gripping the waistband of her shorts, yanking her into me. She gasps and her hands fly up to catch herself against my chest. Her eyes are wide as she looks into mine. I'm not sure what she sees there but I hope it's something she wants. I lean down and skim my nose up the side of her face to her hair where I take a deep inhale of her vanilla scent. I've missed this.

"What are you doing?" she whispers.

"What I've wanted to do since that door hit you in the face the night I got back to town." I see her throat work so I search her face and give her this one chance to pull away, before I gently grip the sides of her neck and bring her mouth to mine.

WINNIE

Rhett is kissing me. Rhett is kissing me and I can't breathe. He's kissing me and I think this may be bad for me later, but right now I'm going to enjoy the ride. I kiss him back and he groans into my mouth, deepening the kiss. I can taste his coffee from this morning and feel a hand sliding into my still damp hair, the other one going to the small of my back and pulling me tighter against him. I let out a sigh and he pulls back to look at me. He's smiling.

"My memory was severely lacking..." He places another light kiss to my lips.

"Have you thought about kissing me often?"

"Only every day since I turned seventeen." I roll my eyes at that.

"Be real, Holloway. It took everything in my arsenal to get you to even look at me back then."

"It seems you're under the impression that the first time I kissed you was the first time I wanted to."

"Well isn't it?"

"Absolutely not."

"So the night you kissed me when we went camping wasn't the first time you wanted to?"

"Not even close. By that time I had wanted to kiss you for years. That was just the first time I let myself be selfish."

"Years? I don't believe that. If you had wanted to kiss me before, I know I gave you every opportunity."

"Oh I remember. It felt like you were torturing me." he says as he kisses a line from my jaw to my ear.

"Torturing you? You wouldn't even look at me!" I remember trying to get his attention, thinking all it would take to turn his head was a short sundress or sunbathing in his yard. He stops his kissing to look at my face. There's a glint in his green eyes.

"I couldn't look at you, Winnie. Colt was always right there beside me and if he even caught a whiff of what I wanted to do with you, he would have killed me."

"I had no idea you felt that way about me back then."

"I've been thinking about you like this—" he breaks off and brings his lips to mine again, making me feel boneless. "—since your seventeenth birthday, Darlin'. Since you decided to torture me in that tiny orange bikini that made it impossible to look at you without everyone else knowing exactly what I was thinking about." No way he remembered that bikini. My jaw hangs and a laughter bubbles out of it.

"But that was five years before the summer you kissed me by the lake!"

"Mm, my favorite summer."

"Mine, too." I think about not telling him the truth, but I feel like being brave when I'm in his arms like this. "I thought about asking you to forget about our agreement."

"I wanted to ask you to come with me." That surprises me, I take a second to decide if I want to know but the words are out before I can make the decision.

"Why didn't you?" He looks up and his brows pinch before meeting my eyes again.

"You seemed so set on cutting things off. I didn't want to put myself out there first. If I could go back now, I would ask you. I can't go back and change anything, but I can do things differently now." I nod, he kisses my forehead then releases me but grabs my hand to pull me through the house to the front door where his shoes are. I already miss his warmth when he bends down to slip his sneakers on. "I do have to go next door for a while though. I'm meeting Alder and Knox. The rest of my furniture is being delivered today and then I will officially be moving in next door. You know, I didn't buy the house because of it's vicinity to you, but it was a big selling point."

"You knew I lived here before you bought it?"

"My family may have mentioned it the day I signed the papers, the same day you decided to give me a sneak peek in the window." He winks and I laugh loudly at that.

"I didn't know anyone was in the house and what were you doing staring into my window?"

"I wasn't staring into your window, I glanced in your houses direction."

"So, basically you're stalking me?" I tease.

"Yep. And I don't plan on stopping anytime soon." He grabs my face with both hands and kisses my lips in three quick pecks. "Can I see you tonight?"

"Yes." I answer a little too quickly but I can't find it in me to care. He wants me.

"Great. I'll pick us something up for dinner from Knox's?"

"That sounds great. I'm going to go to the bakery for a few hours. I have some orders to catch up on and getting things ready for next week."

"If you need any help, I'm there." That makes me smile. He's always showing up for me.

"I should be able to handle it all myself, but thank you."

"As long as you know you don't *have* to handle it on your own."

"I do and I appreciate the offer. Really."

"Oh, I have plenty of offers for you, darlin'. I'm hoping you'll take me up on a few of them." I smile at that and stretch up onto my toes to kiss him. He kisses me back, gripping my hips tightly before letting go. "I'll see you later."

"See you later." He opens the door and kisses my cheek before stepping out and bouncing down the steps. I shut the door and let out the girliest squeal I have ever squealed in my life. I have wanted this for so long and finding out that Rhett still wants me too, that he never sent those messages to me. It feels so good to let that go, but it also makes me feel incredibly vulnerable.

He wants me now but if he decides I'm not what he wants it will break me. We were together for a summer eight years ago. He may think he wants me, but there's so much that he doesn't know about me. Things he should probably find out before deciding he truly wants to be with me. I need to try and slow down. I take a deep breath and get ready for my day at the bakery.

WINNIE

Kneading dough is therapeutic. It's the perfect time for me to reflect and process. It also really helps with my anxiety. I'm playing around with some new recipes and treats for the special orders next week. Another thing I love about living in Silverthorne is all the events the community comes up with. There's always something happening to take part in. I've been to most of them starting with the Autumn Craft Festival at 13. Mary had asked Uncle Buck if she could show me and Colt around with her and Rhett while he was running his chili and beer booth there, like he does at most town events. She had bought me kettle corn and I remember smiling for the first time in months at hearing Colt laugh for the first time in months. I may have started falling for Rhett for that reason alone. When she dropped us back off with my uncle she gave me the small purple mesh pouch.

"You're a lovely girl, Winnie. I hope you'll be happy here."

My throat feels a little tight recalling her words that day and my fingers automatically go to my wrist, the wooden beads make a light knocking sound as I fidget with them. She had given me the bracelet I had admired at a local jewelry booth that day. It made me feel cared for and special. Something my mom had always managed to do so well, that I didn't realize how much I would miss it until she was gone. My uncle is a wonderful man, and had taken us in without a thought. He's kind and funny and he showed Colt and I love that I could have only wished for after losing our parents.

There was just something about having a woman care for you in the most thoughtful ways that we tend to care for one another. Mary had never let me feel less than one of her own. Would she be disappointed in Rhett and I? If things with us didn't work out would I lose her? The whole Holloway family? That was a big risk. I relied on them. Loved them. Something else to add to the list of topics to cover tonight. It's so easy to get swept up in him when he's next to me, invading my space and scrambling my brain. I look down at the bread I'm kneading. It's time to get it into the proofing drawer before I add the strawberries to it. I set a timer for two hours and call Mare. She has sent me a handful of texts this morning but I needed to process this on my own for a while—now I need to talk to someone about what happened this morning. It only rings once before she picks up.

"Winnie! How are you feeling, babe? You haven't answered any of my texts!" I can hear beeping in the background and squeaky wheels so she must be at work.

"I'm sorry, I'm fine. I was...a little busy this morning." I hedge.

"Busy? With what? The bakery?"

"Among other things..."

"Put me out of my misery here!" I let out a long breath.

"I kissed Rhett this morning...or he kissed me. We kissed." Silence. Then I hear rustling, quick footsteps, a door closing, and finally a ridiculously loud scream right in my ear.

"Shut up! Shut up, shut up, shut up!" Pull the phone away from me at her shrieking.

"I'm not saying anything." I laugh.

"Well start talking! What was he doing there? How was it? Better than you remember? What does this mean for you guys? Will there be a repeat?"

"Um he came over last night and ended up staying the night." She gasps and I rush to add. "Just to take care of me."

"Aww, Win. That's the cutest thing. So he stayed the night...where does the kiss come into play? I thought you were still upset about what happened a few years ago...?"

"Well it turns out that he never got my messages that night. You remember Lacey? The girl that Colt had met?"

"Uhg, yes. Colt did not have a good thing to say about that one."

"I'm thinking he was justified in that now, because she was the one that text me back that night." Another gasp.

"No. No way. She didn't."

"Apparently, she did. Rhett read the messages on my phone this morning after I had a small meltdown over him calling me *adorable*...and it was pretty obvious that he hadn't seen them before. He said he had no idea I was there that night and she had asked to use his phone."

"I'm...well that changes things."

"Yeah...it changes a few things...but not everything..."

"Oh, Winnie. I wish you could get out of your own head about this. I can tell you're already thinking about the what if's..." She knows me so well. I smile at that. It's comforting if not a little annoying. I sigh. "Maybe just try to enjoy this? For me?"

"I promise to try. I want to, Mare. I want him."

"I know you do. So maybe let yourself be happy for a minute before you bring any other emotion into it?"

"Okay, I will do my best." She laughs.

"Oh, shoot. I'm being paged to the ER. Gotta go. Love you!"

"Love you, go save some lives or whatever." She giggles while hanging up.

I'm feeling less anxious now. Mare's right. I should just take this one step at a time, not jump to the ending that I've made up in my head. I check my timer and sit down in my office in the back to get my orders in for next week. I still need to go to the berry patch in Brighton. One of the special orders next week is four mixed berry pies and strawberry cookies for a birthday party. I'm going to need some help with getting all the berries that I'll need. I can ask Anna and maybe she'll bring some friends. My timer goes off and I mix in the strawberries and shape the loaves. They'll need another 30 minutes prove after that, then bake for 45. That puts me leaving here at 6:15ish...hopefully Rhett's busy until then. I'd like to change and clean up before seeing him and maybe brush my teeth, the thought has me feeling butterflies swarming in my stomach.

I get home only a little later than I wanted to. Rhett text me to say he was planning on being here at 8. Plenty of time to clean up before he gets here. When I walked by his house, the lights were on. It's a little surreal that he will be living there now, sharing a fence with me. I spend a lot of time in my yard, so he'll be seeing a lot of me when he's home.

Hopefully that will be a welcome sight. I change out of my leggings and baggy shirt into jeans and a fitted t-shirt, deciding since we're going to be at my house that I should be casual but not in sweats...? Although why not sweats? It's not like Rhett hasn't seen me in them. Or a swimsuit. Or practically naked the other night, or actually naked so many years ago. *Stop Winnie.* Sometimes I can spot a spiral before it happens. Sometimes I can't. Tonight I'm not going to spiral. We haven't even talked about anything yet. When you've wanted something for so long, It's hard to accept that you might be getting it. I hear a knock and take a breath before walking to the front door.

"Hey. Come in."

"Hey." He breaths out and sets the bags of food on the floor by our feet. He grins and then covers my body with his in a hug. He smells good. He kisses my temple.

"I've been waiting to do that all day." I blush.

"How was moving? Did you get everything settled?" He nods.

"I did. We are officially neighbors. A quote in a different language?" His smile is so big. He looks so happy. "Are you hungry?"

"Starving and nope, that's a good guess though." it's the truth. I only ate two croissants and a blueberry muffin today.

"You should have eaten the breakfast I made." He winks.

"I should have. Instead I had a mini meltdown. It was really sweet of you to cook for me, though." He chuckles and kisses my cheek.

"I'm not unhappy with how the morning turned out." He picks up the bags and walks to my kitchen table.

"What did Knox make us?" I ask following him. Knox may be a lawyer but he's the best cook of all the Holloways, besides Mary.

"He made us chicken gnocchi with pesto cream sauce, garlic knots, smoked brisket, mac n' cheese, apple pie, and a blondie brownie with maple pecan sauce. I got some vanilla ice cream at the store." I'm stunned.

"Those are all my favorite foods."

"I know. I didn't know what you would be in the mood for so I got us options."

"You remembered all my favorites?"

"I remember everything about you, darlin'." I launch myself at him. I kiss him with all the longing that I've held inside. He catches me and kisses me back just as wildly. I'm close to him but not close enough. When we break apart he rests his forehead on mine.

"I would have brought you food a hell of a lot sooner if I knew this would be your reaction." I laugh.

"It's not the food, Rhett."

"I know, but I will bring you food every day if you'll let me." I smile and kiss his soft lips once more before pulling away. Every day is sounding really good.

"I may hold you to that. Now let's eat. I'll grab some plates." He stops the movement by pulling me in again and kissing me hard.

"I missed you." I roll my eyes at that.

"Yeah? Seeing me this morning wasn't that long ago, you know?"

"I'm not just talking about today." Those butterflies are loose again.

"Obviously. I'm really easy to miss." He barks out a laugh at that and kisses me again.

"Okay, let's eat now. I wanna hear more about your day." I get the plates and we fill them. "I meant to tell you earlier but you've done a really amazing job with this place, Winnie. I love the tiles and the floors look great." I blush at his praise but I am really proud of myself and all the work I've done here.

"Thank you. I have a few more things on my list to get to but with the bakery I've had to put a pause on the renovations."

"What's left on the list?"

"Well, I still want to switch out the fixtures in the bathroom and I need to replace the vanity in there, too. I have the piece I'm wanting to use in my shed but I just haven't had time to set the sink in it...the biggest thing I have left though, is re-painting the exterior."

"Why haven't you done that yet? Wouldn't you hire out for that anyway?"

"Yeah, I would, but I don't quite have the money for it yet. I'm thiiisss close..." I hold up my hand and pinch my fingers together. "Doing most of the work myself has saved me a ton, but it still costs a lot to renovate." He nods thoughtfully.

"What color are you thinking?"

"White."

"It's already white." I smile.

"How observant you are, Rhett." He smiles at my sarcasm. "It is, but it's old and chipping. Discolored in some places. It needs a spruce. When I bought this place I loved it, but one of the things I wanted to do is breathe some life into it."

"You're doing a good job of that. I see you all over in here. I may need you to help me with my place. I love it, but it's extremely dated on the inside. I need someone to help me update and customize it."

"I would love that. Seriously, if I hadn't decided on baking as a profession, I think I would have gone to design school."

"You would be successful at anything you want, Winnie."

"And there's that charm I've always been so weak for." He laughs, shaking his head.

"That is one word that I could never use to describe you. You're one of the strongest people I've ever met." That brings me up short. I get uncomfortable with compliments. Even more so with ones I don't believe have any truth to them.

"You don't have to say things like that to me ya know?"

"I wish you could see how strong you are. How absolutely fierce you can be."

"Fierce? No. That's not me at all. Mare is fierce and fiery. I'm an anxiety ridden, clumsy wallflower. That's not to say I'm not amazing. I know my worth. I just also know myself." He's shaking his head again, but this time he looks a little annoyed.

"It wasn't my intention to argue with you, Rhett...I just know who I am and I'm okay with that."

"After everything you've been through, you still manage to brighten the day of everyone around you. Even when your anxiety is running so high that it's physically affecting you, you show up for the people you care about." My face is hot and I'm not sure what to say but he keeps going. "You're incredible, Winnie. You fight through your trauma and pain and turn it into light and warmth and share that with others. You have so many people who witness your strength daily." I swallow and it feels thick.

"Thank you. For seeing me."

"You'll all I see. You're all I've been able to think about

since I got back to town. I'm in this, Winnie." Hearing that is simultaneously what I want to hear and also scares the shit out of me. I want to tell him I'm in this, too. I'm just scared that I'll lose so many people if he outgrows me. I go with complete honesty instead.

"I...I'm not sure I can be everything you want, Rhett. I have issues. I'm going to mess things up at some point." He cocks his head and studies me, then bends to the floor in front of me. I fight my flush but it's useless. He takes my hands in his and starts playing with my fingers as he speaks.

"You are exactly what I want and everything I've been missing in these years I've spent without you." I guess blushing is just top priority tonight.

"I've really missed you, Rhett. I want to give this a real try." He smirks.

"Did you think I was going to give you choice in the matter?" Laughter shakes loose from my chest.

"I didn't have a choice either way." His smirk softens to a shy smile. I love this look on him. He leans up and catches my mouth with his, ending our kiss too briefly for me. After he sits back at his chair, we eat the very thoughtful meal he brought over. I laugh and feel myself get even more wrapped up in him and that dimple.

I go to bed thinking about him. About how much I want to be with him. He asked me to go on a hike with him this week. I don't really have the time...or the coordination, but I said yes. There's not much I can do when he says please and flashes the grin that makes his dimple pop. Yes, I want Rhett. Badly. I'm just left with the question that it always seems to come back to. Will this be worth the risk in the end?

RHETT

I'm getting my gym bag ready for practice and smiling about seeing Winnie later today. Two weeks ago I kissed her and told her I wanted to be together. We've spent almost every night together since. I'm looking around my bathroom at various hair scrunchies and clips, smiling. I love having little things of hers here, in my space. I know it's only been two weeks but she still hasn't told her brother and I'm starting to feel guilty about hiding it from him. I had to make up an excuse last week when he asked to go rafting because I had already made plans with Winnie. I would bring it up to her later and see where her head was at. I want this out in the open. I want to kiss her in the middle of town and hold her hand walking into my parents house.

Getting onto the ice is feeling better since my first skate a few weeks ago. My knee is still bothering me, but it's much more manageable. I'm here a little early to warm up. We have our first game in a month and we're looking good. I'm really proud of this team.

"Hey, Coach!" I look up from our schedule to see my goalie walking in.

"Bruner. How's it going?" His answering smile is so cocky it makes me start shaking my head already.

"I'm me, coach." Both his hands point at his chest. "It's always good when you're me." I should probably put him in his place but he needs this attitude in the long run. A goalies ego needs to be huge if they're going to keep that puck out of the net.

"Let's get you out on the ice then and see if your answer changes."

"You got it, coach!" My other players start making their way into the arena then. I'm excited to get them all out here and see how our progress is coming along. There's been a little pressure put on me, coming off a professional hockey career. There's been plenty of support, too. This town is just itching for a win and I want to make sure they get it.

We have about 10 minutes left of a decently grueling drill I'm having them work through when one of my wingers lets out a low whistle. I give him a look, follow his line of sight and then blow my whistle.

"You all can hit the showers! I'll see you next week, we have five more practices until our first game, let's make sure we're giving them all we've got."

"Yes, coach!" They say as a group. When I turn back around she's leaning against the half wall smiling at me.

"Hey, coach," she calls in a voice that can only be described as seductive. I grin. I think she knows how much I like that. I skate over to her full tilt, sending ice flying when I stop.

"Ms.Parker, it's always a pleasant surprise to see you, but what are you doing here?"

"I was dropping off some pastries and coffee for the teachers and thought I would come see your coaching abilities in action. It did not disappoint, Coach Holloway. You're pretty good at this." My chest warms at her compliment.

"Thank you. High praise coming from you." She tilts her head and looks innocent.

"Is that something you're into?" This woman is gonna give me a heart attack.

"I'm into pretty much anything if it involves you, darlin'." She smiles widely and leans further over the wall.

"I can't wait to hear more."

"I'm all too willing to spill the details." I say as I wrap my arms around her waist and lift her up. She lets out a surprised laugh and then settles her legs around my waist.

"Do not drop me, Rhett."

"Never, darlin'." She kisses my cheek and I skate us to the other end of the rink and sit her on the edge of the bench so I can take my skates off.

"Let me change really quick and we can get out of here."

"Sounds good, coach." I shoot her a look that hopefully conveys the depth of my feeling.

"Knock it off or we're only going to make it to my office." She blushes but then her sweet honey eyes take on a very flirty glint then sighs.

"Whatever you say....coach."

"Alright that's it." I get my last skate off and grab her by the backs of her thighs and put her over my shoulder, giving her a smack as she giggles and kicks.

"I'm sorry. Put me down before one of us gets hurt. You know I'm uncoordinated enough to take us both out." Laughter barks out of me at that.

"Winnie, do you really think I would let anything happen to you?"

"It wouldn't be your fault." I clear the door to my office then and sit her down on the middle of my empty desk, turn and lock the door. I put my back against before speaking to her.

"Now, do you wanna try that again?" She's still pink cheeked and flustered. "Don't get shy on me now, darlin'." Her back straightens and her eyes harden at the challenge as I walk over and place my hands on either side of her on the desk and kiss her neck below her ear.

"I'm not sure what you mean, co—" She doesn't get the full word out before I bring her mouth to mine and kiss her, unrestrained. She moans into my mouth and I bring my hands up to her face, one tangling in the hair at the nape of her neck. Our kissing quickly turns heated and her hands are exploring my torso under my shirt, I'm dizzy. I pick her up to switch positions, now I have her straddling me on my desk and I don't think I've ever wanted anything more in this moment. The sounds she's making and the way she's moving against me are enough to drive me insane. I pull my mouth back from hers just for a minute.

"Winnie..." She's kissing down my neck and reaching lower between us so I grip her wrist to stop the advance. I need to think straight.

"Winnie..." She looks at me then.

"What? What's wrong?" Wrong? This situation is something. Wrong is definitely not the word I would use.

"If we keep going like this, I'm going to end up taking you here and now in the coaches office."

"I'm aware, Rhett." She's killing me.

"I want you. So badly, but after all this time. I want you in my bed first. Not here when someone could come knocking. I want to take my time with you." She smiles.

"Okay." She goes to climb off me laughing but I wrap my arm around her back.

"Just give me a minute darlin'." She giggles and snuggles her face into the spot between my neck and shoulder and I hug her close. I laugh with her.

"It's good to know that even if other things have changed, these feelings haven't."

"None of my feelings, along with these ones, have ever been in question." She looks in my eyes for a moment then kisses my lips softly. "Song lyrics?" I ask, I won't give up until I guess this tattoo cover up.

"Good and no, not song lyrics. Now, let's get out of here. I'm starving." I let her down then and adjust myself before finding my shoes.

"We better get you some food then. You get mean if we wait too long."

"I do not get mean! I just need plenty of protein to fuel this enchanting personality you love so much." She smiles sweetly at me and I reach into my bag and pull out a big ziplock baggie labled "WINNIE SNACKS" and toss it to her.

"Pick something to hold you over." I call as I lace up my shoes. When I don't hear her getting anything out I look at her. Her eyes are glistening.

"Hey, whats wrong?" She swipes at her face then clears her throat.

"Nothing. You carry a bag of snacks for me?"

"Yeah, I noticed when we were hiking a couple weeks ago that snacks are a must for you, that hasn't changed in the last eight years." I give her a wink.

"That's the most thoughtful thing anyone has ever done for me, Rhett. Thank you." I walk over to her and hold her close.

"It's just snacks in a bag, Win. It's only a small fraction of the things I would and will do for you." Her smile is so sweet when she looks up at me.

"I have a list of things you can do *to* me—" I fake a scandalized look and drop my mouth open.

"Ms. Parker!" I admonish.

"—just so you're aware." She grins and I kiss her mouth once more before taking her hand and pulling her from this office before things start warming up again.

WINNIE

I'm up early and in the bakery today. I have so much to get done this week. We have orders for five different events this weekend, which is amazing, just a lot for my small bakery. I have been just a tiny bit more distracted then normal lately. Not that I'm complaining. Rhett is a very welcome, very hot distraction. I can feel my smile and touch my face. I haven't smiled this much in a really long time and I know...it's new, but it feels like it's been building over the course of half my life. I'm taking a page out of Mare's book and just enjoying myself. I am really enjoying myself. We've spent a good amount of time getting to know each other physically these past few weeks and if you ask me it's not enough. That man is pure tattooed muscle that I'd like to take a bite out of—

"Hey, Winnie!" I'm jerked out of my daydream by Anna calling my name at the kitchen door.

"Hey, Anna. Need something?"

"I have someone out here wondering if they can place a

special order. I know you're busy this week but wanted to check."

"Uhm...depends on the order but I can probably swing it." To be honest I've loved being busy this week. This week marks the 18th anniversary of my parents accident and I don't like to dwell on it as much as possible.

"She's wanting some custom cupcakes for her daughter's birthday." She looks at a small notebook in her hand and starts reading. I smile. Anna has really come a long way as an employee. I'm proud of her. "Four dozen lemon cupcakes with raspberry filling and cream cheese frosting. What do you think?" She looks up at me.

"Well...I can get that done and the other things on my list if you think you could help me...?"

"Of course! I can run errands and take of the front of the shop no problem."

"I was actually hoping you could help me in the kitchen."

"In here? Your kitchen? You want me in here...with you?" I laugh.

"Yes. If that would be something you wanted."

"Yes!! Yes, I would love that!"

"Great. Tell her we can do them. When does she need them by?" She checks her notes again.

"She needs them on Friday, so three days. Is that still fine?"

"Yep. I think we can do it." I wink and she beams. I feel bad for not having offered her access to the kitchen sooner. I had no idea she would be this excited. I used to love helping my mom in the kitchen. She was an amazing cook and baker. Then I was able to help Mary after we moved here. My eyes are hot and I can feel tears start but I sniff them away. I can't afford to get off schedule today. I'm going over to Rhett's tonight to help with some design choices and he's making me dinner. I've never had a guy make me dinner before.

It's been a long day and I am exhausted when I get home. Rhett's truck wasn't parked beside his house when I walked by. He must still be at the school. I need to shower and get changed before walking over anyway so I strip my flour coated clothing off and throw it in the basket by the laundry on my way to the bathroom. I look at myself in the mirror and I am a mess. I start the shower and go to my closet to grab some clothes. I decide on some spandex shorts and a big t shirt.

In the shower I wash away all of the various baking ingredients from my hair and body and also let the feelings surrounding this week come to the surface just enough to examine them. Sadness. Grief. Longing. I sit with each feeling for a moment and try to let it go. It's a practice that has helped me for years. It doesn't make the pain go away but it helps me process and keep my anxiety level manageable. I like to end this with remembering that the reason I feel these things is because I had felt loved and cherished. I picture my moms eyes, the same color as mine, crinkling at the corners while she laughs with me. I remember the look on my dads face, arms stretched out and hugging her from behind. I hear his laugh as she swats at him. God, I loved his laugh. I feel a few tears trail down my face and wash them away in the spray of the shower before I turn it off.

I'm dressed and letting my hair air dry when my phone rings. *LOML* pops up on my screen along with a picture of me sprawled out on a picnic blanket next to Rhett that he snapped of us at the lake weeks ago. I roll my eyes and I'm laughing as I answer.

"L.O.M.L. huh?"

"L.O...mm what? I don't know what that means...?"

"So you didn't break into my phone and change your contact?"

"What are you accusing me of, Winnie?"

"Mm must have been another stalker of mine. My mistake. Did you need something?" I grin when he growls on the other end of the line and look out my kitchen window that faces the back of his house. He's already standing in his yard and looking in my window. I gasp.

"Jeezes, Rhett! That scared the shit of me. What are you doing out there, besides being creepy?" He chuckles but doesn't answer.

"I was thinking we should put a gate in the fence here so we can go between yards."

"Why? You can just use the sidewalk right there." I point towards the street still looking at him.

"Yeah, but I like the idea of being attached." I smile then he adds... "Dreamcatcher?" What?

"Umm...I know we haven't discussed pet names but that one isn't really doing it for me." I step out the side door of my house and walk towards the fence, hanging up. His laughter is loud and undiluted. I love it.

"Your tattoo cover up. Dreamcatcher?"

"Are we still on this?"

"Until I guess it, absolutely." He says as I reach the gate. "Ready for dinner?"

"Yes, I'm starving. But I can't stay too long. I have to be up incredibly early in the morning."

"You're always up incredibly early."

"That's true, but tomorrow even more so. I have to go out to the berry patch and pick as many strawberries as I possibly can for the weekend."

"Do you need help?" I wave him off.

"I can manage. Anna is coming late with a few of her friends from school."

"You know I like helping you right?" He reaches over the fence and smooths some hair away from my face.

"Why is that exactly? I'm sure you could find more adventurous things to do."

"I like spending time with you. I like having our own adventures." I bite my lip.

"How did you ever get to be so damn charming?"

"It's not something I can help when I'm with you, Honeybee. Infinity symbol?" I open my mouth to say something sarcastic like *Smooth, Holloway*...but start laughing about the tattoo comment.

"No, no no no." He reaches down and has me sailing through the air again.

"Why are you constantly picking me up?" I'm always giggling with him. He makes me feel so light and carefree.

"One: I like touching you. Two: I love hearing that giggle. Three: It makes me feel very strong, because you are so tiny." He laughs and carries me into his house.

"You know, I thought when I came over tonight I would use the front door and be upright."

"Why would you think that?" I smack at him but he sets me upright before I can make contact.

"It suspiciously doesn't smell like food in here. I was promised dinner." I muse.

"About that...I was going to cook for you...." I put my hand on my chest.

"...but...?"

"But, I was working on a side project after I got done at the school. I really did plan on cooking. Next time I will."

"You know, I was all excited because I've never had a guy cook for me but—I guess you're just like all the others..."

"The hell I am." I laugh.

"Easy, big guy. I'm joking." He raises his brows at me.

"Well I'm joking about you being like all the other guys..." I see the look on his face and smile. "...but I wasn't joking about how hungry I am. Do you want me to make us something?" He looks horrified.

"Winnie. Do you think I would invite you over just to ask you to cook?" From the way he just asked, I figure telling him that I cooked for my last boyfriend most of the times we were together isn't the move.

"No...?"

"Well, I didn't. I ordered from pizza from Mix's." I gape.

"I love Mix's." He chuckles.

"Which is why I ordered from there. Carpe Diem?" My smile is wide.

"Not even close." I taunt.

"I'll figure it out eventually." I shrug.

"Maybe. Now, are you going to show me what projects you're thinking about? I'm kind of excited about starting a few over here."

"Come on then, Honeybee." He starts for the staircase and I trail behind him looking around me. "We'll start with the upstairs and work our way down. What about a book quote!"

"Perfect and no, why would I cover up a book quote?" I follow him around from room to room only making a small detour in the master suite. If he really lets me loose in here there is so much potential for an absolute masterpiece. We make it back to the kitchen before he really says anything.

"So, what do you think?"

"Rhett, it's beautiful. I love it! I honestly can't wait to get my hands on this place."

"I can think of some other places I wouldn't mind those hands." He winks, but before I can think of a reply he continues talking about the house. "I know I want to change out the tile in the kitchen. I loved the green tile you had in yours. I also want to change out some fixtures, maybe just refinish all the doors but keep the hardware. A black cat?"

"I love all those ideas, I think I would go with a slightly darker green in your kitchen. And no, but honestly I would like to get one." I grin and his phone starts ringing from upstairs where he left it after showing me how comfortable his bed was.

"I'll be right back." He kisses my lips and races back up the stairs when the doorbell rings. "My wallets on the island! I have cash!" He yells down. I walk around the island, grabbing his wallet as I walk toward the front door. I open and smile at the delivery guy.

"Hey, how's it going?"

"Good, can't really complain." He hands me the pizzas. "Total is $29.63."

"Right..." I set the pizzas on the desk by the door and in the process drop Rhett's wallet onto the floor and spill the contents. Oops. How very on brand for me. I grab the wallet and start picking up some cash to pay this poor guy so he can get on with his night, but I freeze when I see a crinkled photo amongst the scattered coins and dollar bills. It's me. From that summer. I'm sitting in the back of Rhett's truck with his Silverthorne hockey sweatshirt on and my hair piled on top of my head, a sweatshirt

I still have and is very well loved. The same one he saw me in the night of the accidental strip tease. Pizza guy clears his throat and I grab a $50 dollar bill and hand it to him still kneeling on the floor.

"Have a good night, keep the change."

"Thank you! Have a good night!" I hear the glass door shut but just stare at the photo. I can't believe he has this or that he kept it for this long. I hear him finishing up his conversation as he comes down the stairs.

"Love you too, dad. I'll be out next week to help load up. Bye."

"Win? Are you okay? Did you trip?" He smirks.

"Uh, actually no. I just accidentally dumped your wallet out, trying to pay the pizza guy. I uh...I found this." I hold up the photo and his eyes widen a little.

"Ah. That photo." He scratches at the back of his neck.

"Yes. This photo. Of me." I shake it a little and he walks over and gently takes it from me, shutting the front door, then sitting next to me on the floor. I just gawk at him.

"You kept that." I swallow. "I didn't think you...I..."

"You didn't think what?" His jewel toned eyes blaze into mine. "You didn't think I was so gone for you that I would print a photo of you out at a drug store? So that when I went back to college and was missing you so much I could keep you with me everywhere?" My throat feels too tight. My nose is stinging and my face feels wet. I cough out a sob.

"The reason it's so beat up is because I kept it in my hockey gloves until recently."

"Hockey sticks." I get out somewhere between a gasp and sob.

"What?" The confused look on his face is adorable. "Is that

like some kind of safe word? We never discussed that..." He reaches over and wipes my cheeks.

"No, you idiot." I'm laughing but also crying. "The tattoo... it was hockey sticks."

"You got hockey sticks tattooed on you?" I nod.

"I was gone for you too, Barrett Holloway." He smiles and yanks me forward, kissing my face, my cheeks, my eyes, my throat and then my mouth finally. He kisses me deeply and longingly. Our tongues tangle and then our limbs. We're still on the floor but I don't care as I pour all the feelings I've been holding back into this moment. He wanted me just as much as I wanted him. The information is banging around in my ribcage or maybe that's my heart about to beat out of my chest. I pull back and look at him. We both start laughing.

"And to think if one of us had just said something back then..."

"Who knows what would have happened then. We have now though." He kisses me softly again then grabs the forgotten pizza box from the desk beside us.

"We have now." He says and we sit on the floor in his entry way and eat pizza, without even realizing it I'm teetering on the edge of a cliff, knowing Rhett will be there if I allow myself to fall. I just have to decide if I can.

ℛHETT

I watched Winnie walk by my house through the blinds in my living room this morning and some people, most people, would say that it's creepy. I would agree with them under different circumstances but it's actually romantic in this case. I'm painting her house today. She told me last night when I was over at her house, for the third time this week, that she would be busy all day today preparing for all her special orders this weekend. The team and I went with her to the berry patch yesterday to get all the strawberries she could possibly need.

They didn't complain once, but I did have to give a couple of them a look when they stared at Winnie just a little too long. I couldn't blame them. She had looked beautiful like always, but she had on these tiny little denim shorts that showed off her tan legs. She was wearing an adorable sunhat that I had to lift up every time I wanted to steal a kiss from her. It's hard to say I was stealing anything when she was all too willing.

The thought has me smiling as I grab the 5-gallon bucket of

white paint I bought last night and all the tools the guy at the store told me I would need for the job I was taking on. I could have hired a company to do this but I just really wanted to do it for her. I wanted her to think of me when she looked at it. To be forever stamped on a piece of her life.

I set up my ladder and start using the metal paint scraper on the chipped spots. There are a lot. This is going to take a while. I put in my ear buds and start listening to the book I downloaded after I saw her reading it the other night when we were laying on her couch. She went hiking with me a couple days ago and has agreed to a paddleboard outing next week, so I want to do things she enjoys, too. I also just want to completely immerse myself in her world. I've never wanted to do that with anyone. Just Winnie.

I'm getting to a particularly steamy part of the book that has my ears turning red when I hear a bang. I look below me to see Colt staring up at me with a very confused expression. I take my ear bud out and stash it in my pocket.

"What are you doing to my sisters house?"

"At the moment, I am scraping the old chipped paint off of it."

"Why are you scraping the old paint off?"

"...because I'm going to paint it."

"Huh...okay." He scratches his head under his ball cap. "I'm wondering if you can guess my next question." I'm wondering how Winnie would want me to approach this. We haven't discussed us telling Colt we're together yet. I know she wants to be the one to do it, even though I would like it to be me. I don't think I want to tell him right now though, not while I'm up on a ladder.

"She mentioned wanting to do it and I thought I would be neighborly and do it for her."

"Neighborly." He's mulling over that flimsy excuse and he's smart enough to come to a better conclusion so I jump in hoping to sidetrack him.

"Are we getting out on Clear Creek next weekend?" I can tell by the smile that stretches across his face that I have successfully sidetracked him.

"Yeah! Let's do it, man!"

"Saturday morning? I gave the team next weekend off since they've been helping out with community outreach so often."

"Sounds good, I'll ask one of the other guides to cover me." His phone rings and he digs it out of his pants pocket and checks the name.

"Hey, I gotta get going. Can you tell Winnie I stopped by if you see her? I haven't gotten to see her much lately. She's been busy and I'm worried she may be hiding that she's dating someone again." I choke and try to turn it into a laugh.

"I'll tell her you came by!"

"Thanks man. Catch ya later."

"See ya." That didn't feel good. I wanted to tell him the truth. I want everyone to know that Winnie is with me. I just need to make sure she's on the same page...oh yeah, my book! It was just getting interesting. I had no idea her little cartoon covered books were filled with not so cartoon-ish things. I chuckle and pop the ear bud back in and find my place then get back to work. Her house isn't that big but this is still time consuming.

I'm done scraping and power washing, I have all the windows taped off. I'm ready to start painting. I follow all the instructions for the paint sprayer I bought just for this. I have it

all hooked up and pull the trigger on the handle. To my satis-
faction it works! This is actually kind of fun. That feeling lasts
all of 30 minutes.

I no longer think it's fun, but I am done with the painting. I
just uncovered all the windows and pulled the tape off. I step
back to the black iron gate and admire it. She was right. It looks
so much better with a new coat of paint. Here's one thing she
can check off her to do list. I want to help with all the things on
her list. She makes my life so much better just by being in it. I
want to repay that in some small way.

I grab the string lights I bought for the wood slats over her
small deck in her side yard. I need to get them strung up and
the ferns I bought to hang done before I run home to shower. I
also have to call Knox so he can walk me through how to make
her dinner. I check my watch and it's just after 5. I need to get a
move on if I want this to be finished when she gets home. I can't
wait to see the look on her face, it will be 10x better knowing I
helped put it there.

WINNIE

"Yes, Mare. I am leaving now." Marigold called me about 10 minutes ago to order to me to go home and rest. *Doctors Orders* she said. She loves to pull that card.

"Good. You're going to burn yourself out."

"I just need to get through this weekend and then it won't be as busy. Also, I'm going to hire a part time manager. I already have two interviews next week." I can't believe I am in a place where hiring someone else is even possible.

"That's amazing, Winnie! I'm so proud of you but not at all surprised."

"Thank you. You've been here every step of the way."

"I have. So, where's my cut?" I laugh at that.

"Free pastries and coffee every morning...? Forever? As long as I'm your best friend?"

"Works for me...as long as I'm not being replaced by a certain tall tattooed hunk that you've been spending an awful lot of time with."

"No one will ever replace you. In fact, can we have a girls night next week? What do your shifts at the hospital look like?"

"Yes! I can make Thursday night work. I'm working Friday and Saturday afternoon but I'm free until 2pm Friday. What about you?"

"Thursday is perfect."

"Okay, good. Now go home and rest or make Rhett give you a foot rub." I snort...although that does sound really good. I love his hands.

"Not a bad idea, Ms. Levinson."

"I never had bad ideas, Win."

"Not even when you had the amazing idea to streak through the Jameson corn field and Old Man Jameson came out with his shotgun thinking we were the...what did he say?..." She bursts out laughing.

"The 'critters that keep getting in his garden.'" She belts out and we both start laughing. "Okay not the best idea. I will admit that one."

"Not the best? Mare. We had to cover ourselves with cornstalks and explain what we were doing—four times because Mr. Jameson is hard of hearing." She laughs harder.

"Okay, okay. That was the only bad idea I've ever had and I'm hanging up before you try to tell me there were more. I love you! Bye!" Now I'm laughing.

"Bye. Love you!"

I check my phone. It is now 6:30 pm. Feels about right. I'm starving and don't feel like cooking tonight. It's too late to go beg my uncle for food. I suppose I'll order pizza again. Maybe Rhett will come over, too and I will possibly ask him to rub my feet. They're killing me. I click on his name that I haven't had time to change yet. Yes, that is the only reason, I tell myself.

"Hey! Are you coming home?" He answers after the first ring and it makes me giddy.

"Hi." I like the way he says *coming home.* "Yes, I am. I'm so tired and sore. I was thinking of ordering pizza and vegging out. Want to join me?"

"I would love to but I'm hanging out with Alder tonight. I haven't seen much of him since I've been back, so I said I would go over to his place and have a beer."

"Oh, okay." I try to hide the disappointment in my voice but I cringe because it is still very present. *Since when did I start relying on him this much?* I try again. "That sounds like fun, I'm glad you guys are hanging out." I smile even though he can't see me as I round the corner before our street.

"I'm free tomorrow though. After you get your orders all done, maybe we can get dinner?"

"Of course. I'd like that." I step onto the sidewalk and pass by his house, admiring it. The sprawling yard and twinkle lights he hung over the backyard pergola. I sigh, it really is a dreamy property. I'm almost to where our fences connect, but skitter to a stop as I take in my small cottage. My mouth drops and I make a squeaking sound. It's been painted. The dingy yellowing color has been transformed into a brilliant white, the shutters have been replaced on the front and are now cedar wood. There's flower boxes that match under each window on the front, filled with wildflowers. Rhett's deep voice interrupts my gawking.

"Winnie? Are you alright?" I walk the last few feet to stand directly in front of my now pristine house. "If you don't shut that beautiful mouth you may start catching flies." I can hear him now without my phone and look to my porch. He's sitting on the front steps in jeans and a white tee with damp hair and bare feet. Am I drooling?

"Wh...when did you...? How did you? Today? So fast?"

"I did it today, yes." He grins. My eyes sting. What a beautiful thing to do. What a beautiful man he is.

"Rhett..." I open my gate and walk on the brick pavers toward him. "I can't believe you would do this for me...well I can, because it's a very you thing to do, but It's perfect."

"I would do anything, and I mean anything to see that look on your face." I blush. "Plus, I need to make myself useful if I want you to keep me around." I laugh, feeling weightless. Wrapping my arms around the back of his neck for support, I straddle his waist, playing with a lock of his hair that's curling at his neck.

"There are a lot of ways you could be useful to me Rhett." He smiles and then I add. "—but I'll keep you around because you're fun to look at." He throws his head back laughing so hard that I can feel it shaking his chest and me along with it. He really is a beautiful man. Not just his sharp stubble covered jaw, this face that has my heart skipping beats, or those emerald eyes I want to fall asleep looking into. It's so much more than that. It's how he can erase my anxiety with his laugh. It's how whether he's picking me up and swinging me around or holding me close on the couch watching tv, I feel safe. He's quickly becoming an irreplaceable part of my life. I want his heart—just like he has mine.

I place my hands on his cheeks and kiss him. I try to show him how much he means to me. "Thank you. I love it. So much."

"Anything for you, Darlin'." He kisses me then grabs the

backs of my thighs and stands. "I have one more thing to show you." He carries me inside and it smells like heaven.

"Oh my gosh, Rhett! Did you also cook for me?" He deposits me into a chair in my kitchen and then walks to the oven to pull something out.

"I did. Lasagna. I hope it's good. It's a Knox recipe—unless it doesn't turn out and in that case he said to tell you he had nothing to do with it." I chuckle at that. It sounds just like him.

"I may be getting a little spoiled here." I say it as a joke but I can hear the vulnerability in my voice.

"That's kind of the point, Winnie."

"Right." I smile.

"What's wrong with me spoiling you?" He sets the lasagna on the stove top and leans his hip against the counter. He looks too good in my little kitchen. I wouldn't mind seeing him like this every night.

"Nothing." I laugh. "Really. I'm just being silly." I shrug.

"I'm not buying it. What's up? Is it too much?"

"Not at all! It's perfect! This is all perfect. You're perfect." That's my anxiety disorder for you. I'm either a rambling mess, spilling my guts or I freeze up and can't get out the words I'm looking for. Obviously the first has happened and now I'm blushing the color of the red sauce on the stove. I cover my face with my hands and try to steady my racing heart. Feeling like this, wanting him this much is hard for me. I don't always know how to handle being taken care of. I hear him approach and crouch in front of me. His hands encircle my wrists and pull mine back.

"As much as I'm insanely flattered that you think that about me—I'm just trying to show you how much I care. How much I want you." His features blur with the rush of liquid to my eyes.

"You're doing a really good job." He laughs and pulls me to my feet. He keeps one hand in mine and slips the other around my back, so mine goes up to the back of his neck. I play with the ends of his hair again. Then he starts to sway with me and hum a song that I've loved since I was a little girl. And just like that, I feel more centered. The sound is so soft and sweet that it prompts a memory I haven't let myself think about in a long time. I'm watching from a counter top, two people swaying in a kitchen so filled with love it's like I can reach out and touch it. My dad whispering the lyrics into my moms ear. Her looking at him with her beautiful smile, singing along.

My eyes are hot and it feels like there's a rock lodged in my throat but I smile into Rhett's chest. He starts belting out the lyrics without warning and spins me away and then back into him swaying me to the beat that...well it's a little off but I don't care as I laugh and join in. He da-dums the instrument build up for us, before the chorus to I Would Give Everything I Own by Bread really takes off. We yell the words together and his grin mixed with way he's looking at me feels like home. We sing and dance and kiss in my small kitchen for the rest of the night. As I look at this man that's had me so completely since I was 15 years old, a part of me that was so broken I wouldn't even think about it, heals a little.

RHETT

I'm on my second beer. I was only going to have one, but Colt made me feel a little guilty about trying to go home so early.

"How's it been going with the team? I heard about the mooning incident at the festival." He chuckles.

"Oh yeah, that. For the most part it's going great. That particular one is a little wild but it's hard to be upset when I see a lot of myself in him. He's a good kid but he likes attention. He was also skating laps for it at our last practice though." He laughs.

"You? Wanting attention and basking in the limelight? I never would have guessed." His words are steeped in sarcasm and I shove his shoulder lightly. "But seriously, you settling in with them alright?"

"I am. I didn't know how I would feel, but I actually love coaching so far and we haven't even had a game yet."

"That's great. I'm excited for you man. Does this mean

you'll be staying? I heard you may have gotten a few offers to coach an AHL team."

"Where did you hear that?" And I wonder if Winnie has heard that as well.

"Knox mentioned it when I ran into him the other night. He was talking—well bragging a little about how proud of you he is."

"Well I did get a couple offers, but this is where I want to be."

"Good to know. It's alright having you around I guess."

"Ah, you really missed me huh?"

"Oh, save it for your girlfriend."

"Girlfriend?" I look at my beer. I mean I guess I would consider Winnie my girlfriend, I'd like her to be more.

"I'm assuming you've already found someone to hook up with. You've been back in town for almost a month now." He chuckles. I take a few swallows of my own beer before answering. I don't like lying to Colt.

"Maybe." Well if that isn't 1000% an understatement.

"Ooo...who is it? Do I know her? Probably, everyone knows everyone in town."

"Yeah you know her." Probably better than most people. "It's still new." Ish. I mean technically *this time* we've only been seeing each other the last month or so.

"Hmm...you're playing this a little close to the vest. You must really like her."

"I do." The more I'm around Winnie the more I want to be around her. It feels a lot more than like at this point.

"You're not giving anything away."

"Just not a lot to say yet." There's a ton to say, I just need to talk to Winnie before I can say it. I notice him looking out behind me again with an annoyed expression. I glance behind me and see Marigold walking next to guy, holding onto his arm with both her hands and laughing lightly. When I look back at Colt, his eyes are narrowed and his jaw is clenched. Interesting. He seems like he may be jealous. I know this because that's how I felt the night of Winnie's birthday. I clear my throat.

"What about you? Anymore ladies you've met up with?"

"Naw, I haven't had time really. I've been training three new guides and no one has really caught my eye lately." That's surprising.

"Really? No one?" He takes a long drink of his beer.

"No one I can do anything about." He says, looking out into the slowly dwindling crowd and I know he's tracking Marigold again.

"So, how goes the rafting business?"

"It's good. These last few months have been crazy with all the tourists on vacation, but it will be slowing down soon."

"Yeah, I bet. The water always gets busy that time of year. I can't wait to get out there this weekend."

"I'm glad we're going. I should probably head out. I've got a big group I'm taking out tomorrow so I'll have to get to the outpost early."

"I've gotta get home, too. I have lunch at mom and dads tomorrow and I was late to the last one."

"And Mary gave you hell about it?" He grins.

"Actually no. I think she was just so excited to have me back, but I don't want to push my luck."

"No. You do not. I'll see you next weekend."

"See you then." I clap my hand on his shoulder as I walk by.

When I get home I realize how tired I am and my knee is

starting to ache again. I stayed too late at Winnie's last night, or not late enough—like the whole night. I look out my window to her house. It's dark and quiet. I pull out my phone to send her a text. I'm tempted to send her a 'U up? Text' for a laugh, but refrain. Instead I send 'Miss you. Wish I was with you.' After 10 minutes with no reply I come to conclusion she's asleep.

I go get an ice pack and lay down on my bed. As I feel the bite of the ice sinking into my sore knee, I'm hit with loneliness and longing. I fall asleep wishing that, instead of my pillow, it was Winnie's hair I was burying my face into, letting it tickle my face. When I wake up in the morning it's her honey eyes I want to be seeing.

I grab my phone and check the time, 9am. I'm tempted to go straight over and see if she's awake but then notice I have a message. 'I missed you last night, too. I was wishing you were in my bed with me.' Time stamped 8:15 this morning. She's up. And I don't want to wait another minute to see her. I get up to change into some sweats and a tshirt. I'm out my front door in five minutes flat, no shoes on and I'm at her door in six. I knock and hear her light footfalls. Then I hear a small thud followed by a low curse and smile. She pulls the door open and I'm greeted by the most beautiful scene I've ever had the privilege of witnessing.

She's smiling wide at me, her golden eyes still sleepy. Her hair is mostly down and untamed. I look down to her bare feet, toes painted a deep shade of green, then up her legs to tiny pajama shorts that are barely showing because of the huge sweatshirt she has on. A sweatshirt with my first pro teams logo on the front. I look back to her face again and her cheeks are pink. Perfection.

"Hi," she says softly.

"Turn around." She raises a dark eyebrow.

"What?"

"Please," I almost beg and she gives me an incredulous look but does as I ask. There it is. *Holloway* in big bold letters across her upper back. I like the sight of my name on her more than I ever thought possible. I sweep her legs with my arm and she flails before grabbing onto me tightly.

"Rhett! What are you doing?" Her worried tone turns into giggles and I shut the door with my foot and lay her down on the couch following so I'm laying on top of her.

"Morning, Darlin'." I take a second to study her face this close. "God, you're gorgeous." She blushes and hooks her thighs around me. I kiss her languidly, lazily then with more force. I kiss her until neither of us can breathe and she's humming into my mouth. I'm breathing hard as I nuzzle into her neck and she huffs out a laugh.

"I like how you say good morning." I grin.

"Yeah? You should see how I say good night." I expect laughter but instead I'm met with her stiffening slightly under me. I sit up enough to see her face.

"Winnie, I was only kidding. We'll take it slow this time."

"Maybe I should," she says seriously.

"You should what?" She clears her throat.

"See how you say goodnight." I open my mouth but nothing comes out. "Maybe tonight?" she asks. My mouth goes dry. I don't know if she means what I think she means but I'm hoping I do.

"Please," I say and she laughs then.

"Two pleases in one day. How very polite."

"Polite?" I run my nose up her neck and whisper in her ear. "Maybe later we can see how polite you can be." I feel her shudder and her breathing changes. I slide a hand over her ribcage and she arches into my touch. I kiss her neck and she lets out a little gasp. I love this woman. I love her smart mouth and her laugh. I love that she's clumsy but doesn't let it stop her from doing things. She doesn't let anything stop her and she wants to be with me. The thought of having her has me floating. She means everything to me. I sit up and pull her with me. She looks warm and flushed and a little dazed. I smile and kiss her lips once before standing. Her pout is so pretty.

"I've gotta go do a couple things and get ready for family lunch. I'll pick you up at 11." I lean down and grab her face in my hands and kiss her long and hard then kiss her checks and nose and eyes as she laughs at me.

"Okay, go before I pull you back onto the couch with me." I would let her. In a heartbeat.

"I'll be back in..." I check my phone. "An hour."

"Okay. I'll be ready."

"You better be." I wink and walk towards the door.

"I will be. I'm excited to see your family and really excited to see Hazey." She stands and walks me out, pulling me into a kiss at the door that starts innocent enough but turns into something else pretty fast. I'm panting as I pull away. "I'll see you soon." She grins and nods.

"See you in a bit." I make it to the gate before I look back. She's still standing in her doorway leaning to one side, smiling. I blow her a kiss and she rolls her eyes but then pretends to catch it before shutting the door.

I can't stop the goofy smile on my face. Even after all these years, I still feel like a teenager in love for the first time. Now I need to get a few things from town before I pick her up in...45 minutes. That's not much time so I better hurry.

I am back on Winnie's front porch 47 minutes later. She opens the door before I can knock.

"You're late, Holloway."

"Only by two minutes." She grabs her purse and a tote bag. "I have some strawberry bread to bring." She always has baked goods on hand. I take the bag from her. "After you." She smirks, shuts her door behind her and locks it. She's wearing another sundress with a slit on the side that I want to slide off her shoulders and her sneakers.

"Again with the manners," she says as she pretends to fan herself, so I grab her around her waist as she walks by and kiss her, then slap her ass as she giggles. "Hmm...that was not very polite. I may have to talk to your mom about this." She shakes her head at me.

"Go ahead. See what happens."

"Are you threatening me? And why am I kind of into it?" I toss my head back at that. She's always catching me off guard. It's one of my favorite things about her. I open her door then the back one to put her bag in. I shut hers for her after she's inside and walk around to the driver side. I reach over and put my hand on her thigh and she covers my hand with both of hers.

"Alright, lets get this lunch over with so we can get back here, alone, as soon as possible." She giggles and I want to hear that sound for the rest of my life.

WINNIE

Family lunch at the Holloway ranch is typical. Hazel is napping when we get there so we waited to eat until she got up. Rhett wrestled both his brothers. All ended up on the ground and covered in dirt at least twice. After helping Mary in the kitchen as much as she would let me, I had two glasses of wine on the deck with Florence. Being here is always a reprieve from stress and anxiety, but today I'm reminded of what I could stand to lose if it doesn't work out between us. His family is like my family. And I can't afford to lose any more people I love.

"So how's is going at the bakery, Winnie? I have people tell me all day how good everything from there is." Florence beams at me and I beam right back at her. She's been working so hard to make improvements at the hotel and she's absolutely killing it.

"It's going great, better than I could have hoped. We have even more special order requests coming in daily and I'm hiring another manager to help me with day to day stuff."

"That's amazing! And you've only been open a few months."

"I know. It's hard to believe."

"I wouldn't say it's hard to believe. You've always made things happen for yourself. You're one of the reasons I decided I could run the hotel." I'm stunned. Florence is a force. I'm caught off guard to know that I helped fuel her drive to succeed in any way. It's beyond flattering.

"You could be successful selling leather bags to a vegan, Flo. You're not only that good at anything you do, but also you're the most convincing person I think I've ever met...maybe only second to Rhett." She laughs.

"Thanks, Winnie. That's always nice to hear and especially coming from you."

"Always. And I'm always here if you need anything."

"I know. I've always been able to come to you with anything." I smile at that. She's been like a little sister to me for as long as I've known her and never once did she make me feel like an outsider when I was spending time with her and Mary. I don't know what I would do if I lost this special bond we have.

I'm wrapped in a blanket, sitting on a lounge chair, contemplating this and weighing this information against how much I care for Rhett when he comes to sit with me on the deck.

"Hey, you. You about ready to head out?"

"Yeah, I think so. Just let me make sure your mom doesn't need my help with anything." I stand and lay my blanket over the railing and go to grab my shoes, but notice him staring. I look down to make sure I'm covered and confirm that I am.

"You're beautiful, Winnie." I blush and look around to make sure no one else is listening.

"Thank you." He stands and walks towards me, then leans

in, caging me against the railing. I can feel his breath tickle the side of my face.

"You're beautiful and I can't stop thinking about touching you. It's killing me that I can't show everyone that you're mine." I melt as he backs away. "I'll grab your bags and meet you out front."

"Okay." I stand there a second longer and smile. I really like the sound of being his. I look up and straighten when I see Mary in the kitchen window. I give her a little wave and she smiles knowingly back at me. Well, if I wasn't sure about her seeing me and Rhett, I am now. I slip my sneakers on and lace them up, unsure about facing Mary, but I guess I better go inside.

"Do you need any help cleaning up?" I ask.

"That's alright, sweetie. I can manage."

"Are you sure? You know I don't mind helping."

"I know you don't, you've always been that way, but there's really not much left to do and I think Rhett's ready to head out. I saw that you rode here together."

"Yeah, it just made sense. him being my neighbor now." She looks at me with a very mom look on her face.

"Mhmm...how's that going? Him being next door?"

"Good. I mean, fine. We're both busy." I'm getting more flustered by the second.

"I'm sure you are." She smirks. "Well, I hope you'll be at all family lunches from now on."

"Sure. You know I love seeing you all."

"We love seeing you, too, Winnie. Always have, always will. I'm not sure what happened all those years ago and I don't need to, but I don't want you to stop coming around again. Understand?" I swallow the lump forming so I can answer. I love Mary so much. The thought of losing her is unbearable.

"Yes. I understand."

"Good, now go on. Have a good night." Her eyes twinkle as she says this.

"You, too. Bye." I walk out the front door and Rhett is throwing Hazel in the air in the yard. My ovaries grow heart eyes.

"You got a little drool on your chin there, Winnie." I've been caught. Knox has an amused smirk on his face when I look over.

"Oh, shut up. I was just admiring how adorable your daughter is." He laughs.

"Uh huh...sure you were." I roll my eyes.

"Bye, Knox."

"Bye, beautiful!" he chuckles. I walk down the steps and towards the truck. Rhett sets a squealing Hazel down to run toward me. I crouch down and pick her, twirling in a circle. I kiss her head and she toddles off to Knox at the steps.

"Bye, Hazel baby!"

"Buh Bye!" she says and waves. My heart squeezes.

Rhett is smiling at me and has my door open when I turn around. I run and jump into my seat, smiling back at him.

"Points for style," he says laughing and I grin, taking an imaginary bow.

"Thank you, thank you." He shuts my door and walks to his side, getting in. All I can do is stare at him. I want him. Desperately. Even though I know that giving in to what I want may derail my life if this doesn't work out. Colt told me that he was offered a coaching position with a team in the AHL. He's left before to pursue his big dreams and he could do it again.

Leaving me absolutely devastated in the process. Because that is what it would do to me to lose him a second time.

"What are you thinking about so seriously over there, honeybee?"

"Us," I answer honestly before I can think of a lie.

"What about us?" I guess honesty is the only way at this point.

"Well—I was thinking about it not working out between us." His head whips to me so fast I'm worried he may have given himself whiplash.

"Why would you be worried about that, Winnie?" He sounds alarmed.

"—because Rhett, we've done this before and it didn't." I'm trying to keep my voice steady but I can feel my anxiety rising. "I'm not saying it was your fault that it didn't. It just didn't." He slowly pulls the car to the side of the road and I'm wishing I would have waited to start this conversation. I sigh. "I can't lose anyone, Rhett." I admit. It's my deepest insecurity, the root of where my worry stems from.

"You won't. That was years ago, Winnie. It's different now." I look out the window and out toward the mountains that surround my home and everyone I love.

"We may be different, but the stakes are still the same."

"So are you saying you don't want to do this with me?" he says it quietly but when I chance a glance at him his jaw is clenched tight. I look away, growing frustrated, too.

"No. I'm saying that I want to do this with you so badly that it's all I can think about! I've been in love with you for over a decade, Rhett. You're all I've ever wanted. I just need you to know what I stand to lose if you decide to leave again." I look back at him but he's smiling so widely I wonder if he's been listening to me at all.

"What the hell are you smiling about? Did you hear anything I just said?"

"I heard everything you just said. I'm just choosing to focus on the part where you told me you're in love with me." I meet his eyes. His beautiful sea-glass green eyes. I wasn't planning on saying that, but I can't deny that it's the truth. He hooks my knees to slide me over the bench seat and cradles the back of my head in his hands.

"You just said you've been in love with me for over a decade." He stares so deeply into my eyes I feel naked. Stripped of all the the sarcasm and humor I hide behind. He looks at me and I feel seen. I'm not used to being so exposed. I'm always pushing people away when they get too close to the real me, but Rhett has seen me. The real me and he wants me. I want to be brave for him. I want to be brave for myself. I swallow.

"I did," I say barely above a whisper.

"Then we can figure the rest of it out," he says and kisses my lips softly.

"Do you promise?" I hate that I sound clingy. "I don't want to lose you again, Rhett."

"You're not going to lose me, Winnie." He brushes my hair back from my face, curling in behind my ears softly. "I don't think I could ever love anyone or anything the way I love you." My heart swells and my eyes sting. I kiss him. Melting into his arms and the promises he's making. Whatever happens, knowing he loves me even half as much as I love him, will make it worth it.

WINNIE

"Do you want to cook tonight or do you want me to pick something up when I'm done here?" Rhett's voice asks from my phone that I left on the kitchen counter as I flip my laundry. He had to go down to the school for a few hours this afternoon and talk with the principal about something to do with media. I guess when you're just coming off one of your most successful years as a pro player people want to know what you're up to. I don't blame them.

"I don't mind cooking." I hear him breath out a long sigh.

"I meant together Winnie, always." I smile.

"You know, you're really good at this teamwork thing. Have you ever played organized sports? Thought about coaching?" He chuckles at that.

"The thought might have occurred," he says dryly.

"Well run with it, cowboy." He laughs again. He always makes me feel funnier than I am. It takes some getting used to but I think I wouldn't mind getting used to it.

"Will do, Darlin'. I'll pick up something and see you in a couple hours."

"Sounds great, see you then. Bye, Rhett." I hang up the phone and can't stop the smile and giddy feeling spreading inside my chest. I'm nervous but excited at the thought of Rhett staying the night tonight. We may have spent the last few weeks at his place or mine, but we haven't slept together yet. On more than one occasion the opportunity presented itself and at the thought of being with him again my skin feels like it's on fire. I know he's been with women in the last eight years, I've been with other men, but being with him just means more.

I don't think I could ever love anyone the way I love him, but I do know I wouldn't want to. When he told me he loved me today it was like I knew the words before he said them and at the same time had been holding my breath waiting to hear them. This man will be the only exception to the rules I made for myself about love, so I want it to be right and I don't want to mess it up. Just as soon as I've felt happier than I can ever remember I can feel my anxiety start to rise and reach for my phone deciding I may need some help.

"Hello?"

"Hey, Mare."

"What's the matter?" She asks. She's always the one to cut right to the heart of the matter. I feel my lips wobble as I struggle to tell her. One of the worst things about my anxiety is that nothing is actually wrong in the moment, I just can't stop thinking about what could be wrong potentially.

"Nothings wrong yet." I get out, hoping my voice is steady.

"Okay, and what is it you're worried could be wrong?" I feel the tears slipping down my face now, not only from the anxious energy in my body making my muscles tight, but also from the deep sense of being known and seen that Marigold has managed to make me feel. She really is the best friend you could ever ask for.

"Rhett's staying the night tonight."

"Sounds like things are going pretty right if you ask me." I let out a small snort. "What specifically are you worried about? Let's list them and work through them." How did I get so lucky?

"I love you Marigold. Thank you."

"I love you more, Win. Now let's get you right."

"What if he can't handle all of me?"

"He seems like he's pretty good at rolling with the punches." I agree.

"What if he takes a coaching job out of state?"

"If that were to happen then you would have a conversation about it, but he's locked into the job he has now for at least a year so it doesn't seem like a worry for now."

"What about Colt?"

"What about him? You should tell him, but your brother loves you more than anyone else on the planet. He'll get on board." I let out a breath at that. Maybe she's right.

"What if he changes his mind?" This. This is the scariest thought I can't seem to bypass.

"Rhett Holloway has been all in on you since you were 22. I don't see that changing. Ever."

"I really hope you're right about that. I'm really stupidly in love with him."

"I know, babe. I'm really happy for you." The sincerity in her voice is comforting and it makes my throat tight with emotion.

"I want to be happy."

"Then be happy, Winnie. Let yourself be happy." I smile.
"I think I will."

"Atta girl! Woo!" I laugh. "I'm walking into work now, but I
expect a full report in the morning. Full, Winnie. I want every
detail." I'm laughing again.

"Okay, go be a hero. I love you the most."

"Never. Bye, Win!" I tap my phone ending the call and get
ready for my evening with Rhett.

After an extensive *everything* shower, spraying the pillow
mist in my room and tidying up the house I hear the door
bell followed by Rhett's signature knock before he lets
himself in. I can feel tension coil in belly. I decided to bake
something for us tonight, not only because I wanted to
contribute in some way to the evening but also because it
helps calm me. I made the strawberry cookies that Rhett likes
and also a loaf of chocolate bread, both are high on his list of
favorites.

"Hey, Darlin'" I feel his arms wrap around my waist from
behind as I'm moving cookies from the baking sheet and onto a
cooling rack.

"Hey yourself." I smile as he nuzzles his head into my neck
and all the tension that was here in his absence melts into
nothing.

"I missed you," he says.

"As crazy as it sounds I missed you, too."

"It doesn't sound crazy at all to me, Winnie. I've spent
enough time away from you as it is." His hands start to explore
my hips and my breath starts coming faster.

"Mm it's nice we can agree on that." His voice is so low and deep as he speaks into the skin below my ear.

"I want to take you to bed. Can we agree on that?" He's driving me crazy as he runs his lips up and down the side of my neck, his words are soft in my ear.

"I think I would agree to anything you asked right now if I'm being honest, Rhett," I whisper.

"Is that so?" His fingers are inching their way up my shirt now. Passing my ribcage until his large hands cup my breasts. I arch into him, wanting contact on all points of my body.

"Rhett."

"Yes, Darlin'?"

"I want you."

"How bad do you want me?" My eyes pop open at his words. I'm thrilled and shocked all at once. I'm on fire.

"Bad," I whine.

"I need to hear you say how much, Winnie."

"I want you so much I can barely see straight, Rhett. I feel like I might die if you don't kiss me." My words are rushed and hard to hear, but he must understand me, because he grips my chin to tilt my head to the side and devours my mouth with his. My heart is beating out of my chest and I can't catch my breath. He's barely touched me and I'm already aching for him.

I turn into him, never breaking our kiss, and he holds me tight against him. Our kiss is pent up passion from the last eight years and need for one another now. The combination is making my head spin. I'm matching him lick for lick and letting my hands explore down the ridges of his stomach, then lower. I feel his hiss when I'm finally under the waistband of his pants, but I don't stop. I want him, have wanted him for years.

Before I get to the place I've been heading for he sweeps

me up and stalks toward my bedroom with me in his arms. I kiss the stubble at his jaw and nip at it. When we enter the room he doesn't hesitate to toss me onto the center of my bed, I bounce once with the motion and watch in stupified awe as Rhett Holloway crawls onto my bed and over me. My blood heats with the look in his eyes. I feel beautiful right now, more beautiful than I may have ever felt in my life. He goes in to kiss my lips again but I put my hand to his chest and he sits back on his heels. I lean up, wanting to be close to him when I speak. I need to know something before this goes further. He's staring so lovingly into my eyes I almost forget my own name, let alone what I was going to ask. I clear my throat.

"I can be a lot to handle, Rhett." I tell him. Trying my best to convey the truth in them. This is his last chance to get out before I fall over the edge with him. I hold his gaze, bracing myself for what's to come. If I'm giving him the out, he could take it and my heart with him in the process.

"Winnie, if you give me the chance, handling you will be an absolute pleasure for the both of us," his says. It's exactly what I needed and possibly the sexiest thing I've ever heard. I launch myself at him, feeling more ready for what's next with him than I ever have.

"I love you," I say between our heated kisses. His answer is one I'll never forget, no matter how wrinkly I get one day, no matter how foggy my mind gets.

"I will love you until my heart stops beating, Winnie Parker. Maybe even then."

With his words, my fate is forever sealed. I'll never recover from this fall. I'll pray I never have to.

RHETT

Last night was the best night of my existence. I've only ever been in love one time and it was with the same woman. Leaving Winnie this morning was one of the hardest things I've ever done. I woke up 20 minutes before my alarm went off and all I could do was stare at her beautiful face so peaceful in sleep. I left her a note and programmed her coffee to start around the time I thought she would be up. When I got back today I would be asking her to move in with me. I never wanted to be apart from her, not even by a small metal fence.

Today, I'm going rafting with Colt and I'm going to tell him about me and Winnie. I'm not sure how he's going to take it or if Winnie will be alright with me taking the lead on this, but I can't hide it anymore and he needs to know. He's my best friend and I don't want that to change. The only reason it would is if he decides he can't be happy for his sister and me.

It's been a couple years since I've done this and I'm excited to get back on the water. I'm picking him up at our take out and driving back up the river where he already unloaded the raft so we can put in. I see his truck as I round the last windy corner of the canyon before I get to our meeting spot. He gives me the finger as a greeting as I pull up to the empty spot beside him. I shake my head but laugh.

"Yeah, you too, man!" I yell out the open window. He gets out of his truck, hops in mine and we're finally on the way. I'm getting pumped. I love this stuff. Growing up here, Colt and I have been on this river more times than I can count but it's always exciting. He pulls out his phone.

"Hey I gotta take this, it's the office." I nod. It's interesting to see him taking care of business. Colt has found a way to make money doing what he loves and that makes me really happy and proud of him. As we're going down the road I'm thinking about how much I've been needing this. I love the rush that comes with trying to work with the rapids, it's the same feeling I get when I'm riding down the side of a mountain on my bike with too much exposure on a techy line. I've been chasing that feeling since I was seven years old and accidentally went down a Black slope on a family ski trip. When I made it down, my adrenaline was through the roof. I think one of the reasons I've loved hockey for so long is for the adrenaline.

Feeling like I'm flying across the ice and no one can catch me is one of the best feelings in the world. Well...it was. I guess it's not gonna be like that anymore. Sometimes the realization that I'm done playing professionally hits me out of nowhere and it feels like I've been injured all over again. I stop next to the boat and Colt already has the door opened, jumping out. I smile and rush to catch up and focus on the present. I want to be here right now and not thinking about the past. I'm shutting the door as Colt comes around the back, then comes up and grabs me by the shoulders. He gets a serious look on his face.

"You brush your teeth this morning?"

"Clean teeth, clean lines!" I say it like a battle cry. It's just a superstition but one we've lived by since we were 16. A guide told us once that clean teeth help you navigate the rapids, we fully bought into it.

"Woo! Hell yeah!"

"Let's gooo!" We get our boat set up and shove off down the river. Clear Creek Canyon is one of the most beautiful places to raft. After a few rapid sessions we hit a lull.

"How's it being back, man? I know it wasn't exactly on your terms, but I am glad to have you back."

"It's good. I mean it's only been a little over a month, but honestly it feels right. I always knew I wanted to come home eventually...my timeline just got sped up."

"I know your family sure is happy you're back." I smile at that.

"It's been pretty great to see them regularly. I didn't realize how much I was missing out on being away. We talked but it's not the same. I've facetimed Hazel once a week since she was born but getting to really be in her life is something else. She's the cutest thing."

"Huh...you know, I know your family means a lot to you, but I don't think I've ever heard you talk this seriously about them. Are you growing up or something?" He snorts. "What's next? A wife and a baby?" I can't stop the image that my mind shows me.

Winnie. I gulp and try to clear my throat before laughing along with Colt. I'm not sure if that's something I should share with him just yet.

"I mean, a wife doesn't sound so bad."

"I didn't say it sounded bad, but it doesn't really sound like *you*." I can't blame him for thinking that. I haven't been a relationship guy since he's known me. A long time. He met Lacey, the only girl I've dated more than a couple months, when I thought things may be getting serious. He wasn't a fan and now I wish I would have taken his opinion a little more seriously.

"Well maybe I have grown up. I've never really tried to make it work long term with someone, but I really think I'd like to."

"That's great, Rhett. Honestly I'm kind of excited to see how this goes." He thinks he's so funny.

"Okay funny guy. What about you? You ever think about settling down?"

"No way, old man. I'm still so young."

"We're the same age, Colt."

"The way you're talkin' has me questionin' that." He can't contain his laughter at that.

I flip him off while he gets a hold of himself.

"Why do I even try?"

"Because I'm the only other guy in this town crazy enough to go do all the crazy things you want to do." I consider that.

"Yeah, I think that is why." He shoves me a little with his paddle but not enough for me to fall out.

"So, how's Winnie doing with the bakery and everything?" I decide to ease into this.

"You know her, she's gonna succeed in whatever she does. She always has." It never fails to amaze me how Colt talks about Winnie. They've been not only siblings but friends for as long as I've known them.

"Yeah, she's always been smart and talented. I remember

she used to always pack the food she made when she came with us to raft or hike."

"Yeah and lay on the bank or hang out at the trailhead," he snickers. "She hasn't gotten any more coordinated. I can't count the times she's gotten herself hurt over the years. I genuinely worry about her some days." I smile.

"I think she's gonna be okay." I'll make sure that she's gonna be okay... I've always been protective of Winnie. She's just someone you want to shield from anything bad.

"I hope so. At least I don't have to worry about her dating."

"How's it been with her dating?" He lets out a short breath through his nose.

"Winnie doesn't really date. She had a boyfriend a month or so ago, and before that she had another one. She's never been one to have multiple dates a week or anything. Thank God she doesn't give every one who looks her way the time of day."

"I bet." That's all I can come up with to say. I don't know how to bring this up, but I feel like maybe I'm not going about it in the right way.

"Yeah, her last boyfriend lived a couple hours away and he was such a dud." He's laughing as he's talking now. "He owned a peach orchard and I know more than I ever wanted to about peaches now, having only talked to him the two times Winnie brought him around." That information helps ease the tension I can feel in my shoulders. I want to ask him more questions, but he's saved from my curiosity by the river. We have a stretch of rapids coming up before take out and we don't want to miss that. I get situated on the right just before we hit the first set. The water is up and running from all the rain this spring so we breeze right through.

A nice thing about having done this run multiple times and

together was that we were like a well oiled machine, we saw the same lines. As soon as we're through we have another session waiting for us. I love when it's non stop and all I have time to think about is my next paddle. We thread between two rocks and catch the eddy turning us around. We haven't seen very many other groups out here today but we've caught up to a kayaker just a little ways ahead of us. We watch as he makes it through the next set with ease and follow suit, but when we look up to find him again, the blue kayak is turned over and its owner is nowhere to be seen.

We get closer to the boat and I'm able to flip it enough to see that the guy isn't inside anymore. We start paddling faster, hoping to find him. I'm scanning the water when Colt starts shouting that he sees him. He's floating downstream fast but we should be able to reach him before the next set. As we go by Colt reaches out to grab him but the guy starts panicking and grabbing onto him and thrashing trying to get into our raft.

"Easy man, we've got you, but you've gotta let me pull you in." No sooner does he get the words out that the guy slips on the side of the boat and then they're both gone. *Shit.* I barely have time to think it before the last set of rapids is on me. I paddle through as best I can but it isn't pretty. Panic is trying to set in but I know I have to remain calm. Colt will be fine. He's literally trained for this. Once I pull off to the side he'll be right behind me. I manage not to fall out and make it to the take out to the left.

I pull the boat up and wade out into the water, watching for them to pop up. Colt's red pfd comes into my line of sight followed by the other kayaker's yellow one and I release a breath. I get the throw line ready and cast it out for them when they come by. Colt grabs it and then hands it to the other guy and they pull themselves in.

"Holy shit, Colt. Are you okay?"

"I'm really sorry, I panicked and pulled you in with me." Yellow vest says.

"Yeah you probably shouldn't be out here alone if you can't handle it." I snap.

"Hey, it's alright, we both made it out of the water, so that's a win." Sounds like him. He's too easy going. "We'll wait for your kayak and help you get it out." I roll my eyes, not as easy to forgive.

"Thank you guys, seriously, I'm really sorry. After I flipped, it just all blurred."

"Hey, it's alright, we both made it out of the water, so that's a win." Colt says again. I look at him then, really look at him. He's smiling and brushing his hands over his wet shorts. "We'll wait for your kayak and help you get it out." That confirms my suspicion.

"Colt, we're gonna have to take you to the hospital. I think you may have hit your head." He pulls his brows together and looks at me.

"I don't think I did, but it got pretty crazy once I fell in."

"Again, I can't thank you guys enough for helping me out." Yellow vest chimes in again.

"Hey, it's alright, we both made it out of the water, so that's a win." Oh jeeze, okay.

"Yep, alright buddy, let's get you into the truck, I'll unhook the trailer and load the boat and we'll get you to the ER."

"Are you sure? I really think I'm fine, Rhett. It's not the first time I've fallen out of a raft, though it has been awhile."

"Yeah, I'm sure Colt. You've said the same exact thing, verbatim, three times in the last 45 seconds."

"Ah, gosh. Now I feel even worse about this." Good grief, this guy again.

"Hey, it's alright, we both made it out of the water, so that's a win." Colt says for the fourth time now. That's not gonna get old.

"Let's go Colt. Get in the truck." He listens to me and gets in. I help yellow vest, Martin tells me, get his kayak and he calls his friend to come pick him up. I unhook the trailer, load the boat, strap it down, and use a lock I find to put on the hitch. I get in the truck and ask Colt multiple questions which he can answer so that's a good sign, I think. I pull my phone out of the dry bag once we make it to the emergency room and they get Colt into a wheelchair. He fights them a little but Marigold is on duty and he makes the smart decision not to fight with her.

"Have you called anyone yet?" She's looking at me.

"Uh no. Not yet. Just pulled my phone out."

"Well you better call Winnie, she'll wanna know he's here." She turns and starts wheeling Colt down a hallway, but calls over her shoulder "After his scans, he'll be in room 13." Great, now I'm calling for the first time today and it's to tell her that her brother is in the hospital with a concussion and I don't know how serious it is yet. Really not what I wanted the topic of our next conversation to be.

WINNIE

When Rhett's name lit up my screen I was so giddy and excited to hear his voice. I was still floating on cloud nine thinking about our night together and what the future may hold for us. Very un-me thoughts. I'm in the back of the bakery, I just got the last batch of pastries out of the oven, so I decide to answer.

"Hey, cowboy." Oh gosh. Did my voice sound as eager to him as it did to me?

"Hey, honeybee." He sounds tense, nervous, not at all what I'm expecting from him.

"Is everything okay?" Here it is, what I've been dreading. He's decided it's not worth it.

"Everything is going to be fine, Win." My heartbeat accelerates and there's a slight ringing in my ears.

"What is it?" I hear him take a deep breath.

"I'm at the hospital." Now my hearts stops. I'm 13 all over

again and losing someone I love. I can't hold the panic at bay and words start tumbling from my mouth.

"Are you okay? What happened? Is it Mary? Tom?..."

"No, I'm fine, they're fine...but um Colt and I went rafting today and..."

"Colt?! Is he alright? Rhett, is Colt alright??"

"Winnie, baby he's okay. He fell out of the boat trying to help someone and I think he hit his head." My eyes sting and I can feel them fill with tears, I can't breathe.

"Breathe, Winnie. Please, baby. He's alright. They're just gonna do some scans to make sure." I'm breathing roughly now.

"Okay..." I croak.

"Moms on her way to get you now."

"Mary?"

"I figured you would need someone to drive you."

"Thank you. I'll be there soon."

"Alright, I'll wait at the entrance for you. He's gonna be fine."

"Right, okay. Bye." I hang up and walk out front. Anna is singing a song and swaying while sweeping. "Anna."

"Yeah, Winnie?" She keeps sweeping.

"Uh, I have to leave." I'm on the verge of tears and my tone gets her attention.

She spins to look at me.

"Is everything okay? Are you crying? What's wrong?" Concern colors her words and show all over her face.

"I....I think it's okay, but Colt is in the hospital and I have to go check on him. Mary Holloway is on her way now to get me."

"Oh my gosh, of course! I'll be fine on my own today and I'll make sure to lock up tonight. Just go."

"Thanks, Anna. You're my best employee."

"I'm your only employee, but I know." I give her a hug and the key to the front door.

"Thank you again, Anna. I'm..." She shrugs.

"I know. Just text me about tomorrow or if you need anything."

"Okay, I'm just gonna grab my bag and wait out front." She pulls me in for another hug and I barely hold myself together.

"He'll be fine, Winnie." She's trying to be reassuring, but she can't know that. No one can. One minute you're planning your family vacation to the beach and the next you're sitting in a white fluorescent lit room that smells like antiseptic hearing that you'll never see the people you love most in the world ever again. I don't trust that things will work out. I've worked every day of my life since that day to make them work out. I see a blue truck pull up to the curb with the Holloway Ranch logo and I run to get in. After I get the door shut I can't get the seat belt to loosen and I start yanking over and over until I feel a warm hand on my arm. I turn and Mary takes a deep breath, I mimic her and she reaches over to help me get buckled in.

"We're gonna get through this, Winnie." I appreciate her not saying everything will be fine. She knows sometimes they aren't. I nod and she starts driving. Fifteen minutes later we're parked. I'm jogging up to the emergency entrance door of the hospital when I see Rhett standing outside. That's when I let myself lose it. He walks towards me and takes me in his arms. I hear an awful wet coughing sound and think someone nearby must be choking, but realize it's me when I feel Rhett rubbing reassuring circles over my back and repeating a calming mantra..."Shhhh...it's okay baby, I've got you." I'm full on sobbing now. Embarrassingly so. I know I should feel that.

Embarrassed—but I can only feel the panic, the anxiety, and memories of a horrible night keep popping up.

"Is he done with the scans yet?" I choke out between sobs.

"He was just getting ready to get sent to his room when I came back out here."

"Okay, I need to see him." He releases me only so far that he has his arm wrapped around my shoulders and he guides us to Colt's room. When we get to the door I stop abruptly and Rhett tightens his hold on me and lets me stand outside for a second. I'm trying to mentally prepare myself for the worst, but a booming laugh startles me. I rush in and start sobbing again. Colt is sitting up in the bed laughing while Mare is looking at his chart and shaking her head at him. Rhett stands at my side, kissing my head as I stare at my brother who I love so much.

"Whoa, whoa...Winnie, it's okay. I'm okay." I move then and with probably too much force, throw half my body over his.

"I w...was ss...so worried, C...Colt." I'm relieved but the adrenaline is making me feel like i"m floating and shaky.

"I'm fine, Win. I stopped repeating things like 30 minutes ago." He smirks. Smirks. "Just had a little spill—no pun intend ed." He winks. "Well maybe some pun..." I glare at him and finally his face softens and turns serious. "I'm sorry you had to worry, Winnie."

"I...I ccan't lose you." He rubs my arms.

"I never want to scare you like this, but it wasn't a big deal. I don't even think I need to be here."

"You do." Mare and Rhett say at the same time.

"Fine, but I've been checked out and I'm gonna be just fine." I look at Mare and she nods.

"He has a minor concussion, thank God he was wearing

that helmet. He'll have to take the next seven days off work and come back in for another scan, but he will be fine, Winnie."

"What the hell happened out there?" Rhett lets out an irritated huff while Colt launches into his big rescue story. I look at Rhett a few times while Colt tells his tale to find him looking at me each time. After he's finished recounting their day on the water, a nurse comes in with discharge paperwork and tells us that someone needs to stay with him tonight to wake him up every two hours.

"Okay, I can do that," I say at the same time that Rhett says "I've got it covered."

"That's okay Rhett, I'll do it."

"You've got to open the bakery in the morning Winnie. I really don't mind and I don't have anything to do tomorrow."

"I should really..."

"I'll text you updates every time I wake him up. It'll be just like you're there." He winks at me then and I relent.

"Okay, but I expect those texts."

"Scouts honor." I'm reminded of the little picture in Tom and Mary's living room of him dressed in a boy scout uniform, he looks adorable when he salutes. A giggle escapes me and it sounds a little manic. I think I'm coming down from my panic and adrenaline induced state. The exhaustion is starting to set in. I hug Mare and thank her for staying with Colt.

"Like I would pass that pain in the ass onto any of my colleagues." We both laugh.

"Hey!" I look at my brother and hug him tight. I know he's okay. He's really going to be okay.

"Call me if you need ANYthing. I mean it. I love you."

"I love you too, sis."

"Mom had to go pick up Hazel for Knox."

"Oh okay, I'll call Uncle Buck to come pick me up." I reach for my phone and he stops me.

"I can run you home and come back for this guy." He points his thumb back at Colt.

"He won't be discharged for another hour, I'll sit with him." Mare offers.

"Aww, I knew you wanted to spend more time with me, Goldie." She throws her pen at him.

"Is that any way to treat your patient?" He sounds genuinely shocked.

"I think he'll be okay." Rhett chuckles.

"I don't know—those two can really go at each other," I say, but I'm walking for the door.

"Love you guys, call me later, Mare!"

"Love you!" They both call, but keep their eyes locked. Rhett put his arm around me again as we walked the hallway. Now that I know my brother is okay, it's starting to sink in that Rhett just saw me have a panic attack and probably thinks I'm a basket case.

"I'm okay now, Rhett. Really." I try to sound more put together than I'm actually feeling.

"I know you are, Winnie. I also know this was hard for you. Harder than it was for anyone else." I tip my face up into the evening air when we make it outside.

The sun is setting, casting neon pink and orange across the Colorado sky. My body is starting to relax and I have no doubt that it's a direct result of Rhett's arm still tucking me close to him. For just a minute I let myself bask in his warmth. The comfort just being with him brings is enough to hold me together right now. He probably thinks I'm going to fall to pieces any second now, but I can't make myself tell him that he can let me go just yet. I soak in his body next to mine and pretend he can hold me close like this forever. I feel like everything has changed in the last hour.

I can't lose anyone. That's the one thought that keeps popping up into my head. I could have lost my brother today and the thought alone, even knowing now that he'll be fine, has me spiraling. I realized after seeing Colt laughing in that hospital bed, that losing Rhett in any way would end me. If you would have asked me last week I may have thought I could keep certain walls in place. If you would have asked me this morning I would have said that I was ready to tear them down completely, but now I know I was flying a little too close to the sun and have been sent back down to earth just for thinking I could hold my own in his orbit.

The lock unclicking lets me know we've made it to the truck. I'm trying to find the courage to do what needs to happen next. He deserves better than this. He deserves everything he wants and it's becoming more clear by the minute that I won't be able to be that for him. I love him. I'll be in love with Rhett Holloway until the day I die. Loving him this much means loving him enough to let him go for good. He opens my door and waits for me to climb in, then proceeds to pull the seatbelt across my chest. The action makes my eyes water, if I let him he would waste all his time on me. He would put everything he has into us and all I would end up doing is breaking us both. Okay, Winnie *please please please* don't cry in front of him again. I'll have to be strong enough for this next part.

"Hey, it's alright now, honeybee." His crooked grin splits the crack in my heart further, but I try to smile back. It's wobbly at best.

"I know. I don't know why I'm crying again. I'm fine, really." I sniff.

"I know you are, but it's okay if you're not." I nod.

"Thanks, Rhett. I mean it. It's been nice to have someone to lean on." He winks.

"Anytime. I'm always gonna be here for you." I give him what I hope is a reassuring smile. By the look on his face I'm not sure it's all that reassuring. "I mean it. You've got me, Winnie." The serious look on his face and the serious tone in which he has used for delivery threatens my resolve. I must have really scared him earlier. I don't want him feeling like he has to take care of me right now. I clasp my hands in front of me and clear my throat from the lump that's forming.

"I know you'll be there for me, Rhett. That's what family's for." The words feel like swallowing acid. He gives me a puzzled look and goes to say something else, but I stop him. I'm in enough pain without having to listen to him be sweet and caring just to tell him we can't be together anymore.

"We had better get going so you can get back to Colt." he steps back from me and shuts the door. I take a few deep breaths and I only have to make it the 15 minute car ride and then I can really let loose the sobs starting to form in my chest. The drive is mostly quiet besides Rhett asking if I'm hot or cold. If I want the radio on. What station I want. Do I mind if he rolls the window down. Honestly, I just want to jump out, but I squash the impulse knowing that the relief from escaping this situation would only be temporary and then bring me more anxiety and I don't think I can take anymore.

Finally after what feels like hours, I'm stepping onto the sidewalk in front of my house.

"I'll text you later with updates on Colt." he says reassuringly.

"Thank you for—everything, Rhett. You are such an amazing man. I've been so lucky to get this time with you." I can tell that my words confuse him a little, but he still gives me a smile.

"You don't have to thank me, baby. I told you, I'm gonna be here when you need me."

The knife turns slightly when he calls me *baby*. This is a new development. He called me that earlier on the phone I think, too. I was too upset to notice, but I definitely notice now. It makes me feel all warm and gooey inside like a chocolate lava cake. Not a bad feeling but one that I know I shouldn't be having right now when I'm trying to put some distance between us. He said something and I missed it while I was in my head.

"Sorry, what was that?" He smiles fondly at me, knowing I was in my head and not voicing what's in it.

"I know it feels heavy right now, but we're going to make it through this and I'm going to be here for you through it..." He says and all I can do is stand there. He looks down at his phone and answers. "Yeah, I just dropped her off and I'm heading back. Keep your shirt on, it's fifteen minutes." He taps his screen then looks at me one more time. "I better get back, Colt is getting restless." I nod and wave, still not having found my voice. I push the door closed and turn for the safety of my house, but hear the truck engine go silent.

"Hold on a second," he calls. I freeze as I feel his arms pull me into him.

"I just needed to hold you for a minute. I love you." I'm paralyzed. Caught between melting into him, surrendering to letting him love me through all of my fears and pushing him away to protect both our hearts in the long run.

"I hope you know what you mean to me, Rhett. I love you more than I ever thought myself capable." He pulls away from me and kisses my lips, soft from the crying.

"I know, baby. I love you that much and more." He gets back in his truck, pulls away from the curb and I stand there till I can't see the tail lights anymore—I'm not sure if it's the distance or the unshed tears that finally cuts them from view. I turn over our interaction in my brain again, something I can't seem to ever turn off. It really sucks that he has to be so great. Getting over him would just be so much easier if he was a jerk.

I sigh and turn to go inside. I'm really looking forward to showering off this day, changing into my pajamas and melting into my bed. As I clear the top of my concrete steps I look over and see the big Queen Anne. He'll be there soon and that means I really will have to leave. I won't subject either of us to any more hurt than I'm going to cause.

RHETT

I've been sitting in my office for two hours. Practice will start soon and I'll have to go out there and put on a brave face for the boys. Truthfully, I'm exhausted. I haven't been able to sleep. I've barely been able to eat or even think about anything, anything other than my current situation. Current situation being that I'm so gone for a woman who won't talk to me.

It's been five days since Colt was hurt while rafting. It's been six since Winnie and I shared the best night of my life. It's been four agonizing days since I've seen her besides a glimpse here and there of her running in and out of her house. She told me she's just busy taking care of her brother and things at the bakery. I know better. I know she's pulling away from me. I also don't know how to stop it.

Colt is home now and resting. We've spoken briefly, but not about what I was about to confess to him out on the water or what he saw at the hospital. I'm not sure if he remembers everything clearly, but I know he remembers me holding

Winnie in the ER. In the few conversations I've had with him he hasn't mentioned her or that he saw me kissing her. I need to talk to him and explain. This isn't like any of my other relationships. I'm in love with her and want to be with her desperately.

"Hey, Coach!" Dusty says as he pops his helmet covered head into my office.

"Hey, Dusty. Ready for practice?"

"Oh, yeah. Just gotta get my skates on. I forgot though, Principal Gordon wanted me to ask you if you would be willing to do that interview you spoke about last week for the town paper. I guess there's a reporter that's been asking." I've done plenty of interviews over the course of my career and been reported on more times than I care for. Usually some sleazeball wants to make me look bad. I assume that's not the case here since it's just the local paper.

"Thanks for letting me know, kid. I'll let Principal Gordon know I'm in."

"Sweet. See ya out there, Coach!" He takes off for the locker room and I'm left with my thoughts again. I'm not sure how to prove to Winnie that I'm here for good. I'm not going anywhere this time. I think it's time I brought in some reinforcements. I'm willing to go to great lengths to get us back on track.

After practice I go by the hospital. I spot Marigold easy enough and make my way over.

"Hey Marigold." She turns and seems a little shocked to see me.

"Rhett. What are you doing here? Everything okay?" She asks.

"Everthing's fine. Well not everything, but I'm hoping you can help me with that part."

"Listen. If this is about Winnie..."

"It is. I'm in love with her and I don't know how to make her see that the only way I'll leave her alone is if she doesn't feel the same way." She smiles at me.

"Winnie is my bestfriend. She's also the most special woman I've ever met."

"We can agree on that," I cut in.

"She's fierce and kind and when she decides someone is worth it, she loves with everything she is."

"So she may not think I'm worth it." It's not exactly a question or something I've meant to say out loud.

"I didn't say that," she interjects. "You've seen she struggles with anxiety—and she's had a pretty big week this last week. She loves her brother and I think it took her back to a place mentally where she was losing her parents all over again. I think it made her think about how allowing herself to love you fully leaves her vulnerable to the pain it would cause to lose you."

"But she's not going to lose me." She shrugs.

"You need to talk to her about that part. You guys haven't told anyone what's been going on with your relationship yet. I don't think she would ever admit it, but I think that makes her feel insecure. Like maybe you aren't telling everyone, because it will make it easier to leave again—or leave her."

"I couldn't leave her. I wouldn't. There is nothing this world could offer me that could persuade me to be without her." She purses her lips and nods.

"I think that is where you should start, Rhett. Show her you're in it for the long haul. I love Winnie, but she can be so stubborn when she's scared. Don't give up on her." I shake my head.

"Not a chance. I won't let her push me away again."

"Good. Now I need to get back to work so—bye. Also, you should go see Colt. He's having a hard time with staying down."

"Right. I will. Bye, Marigold and thank you." She tilts her head and strides down the hallway. I guess it's time for me to have a long overdue conversation with my best friend, but first I send another text to Winnie. *I miss you, honeybee.*

The drive out to Colt's cabin is short, too short. It's not giving me enough time to rehearse what I want to say. I guess I'll be shooting from the hip on this one. I'm pulling into the drive when I see him outside, rinsing off his raft. He's never been able to sit still.

"Aren't you supposed to be resting?" I ask.

"Not really my thing," he calls back and I grin, because that is the truth.

"How's the head?"

"Perfectly, fine." He looks at me then, really looks at me. "I have zero memory loss." Okay so, we are going to be jumping right into this.

"Ah, alright then. Let's hear it." We might as well get this all over with so I can talk him out of throwing a punch at me and straight into being okay with me and Winnie.

"What's going on with you and Win?" Well this is easy enough to answer.

"I'm in love with her." His brows shoot up and he blinks at me.

"You're in love with her." He repeats what I've just said looking at the ground and nodding his head. I stay quiet and let him digest this info. "How long has this been going on?" This one isn't so easy to answer, but I think it's better to stick with honesty.

"This time? Since I got back to town, eight years since the first time I acted on it and in total since I was seventeen." I brace myself. This could get ugly. To my surprise I hear a startled laugh.

"So you're telling me you've been in love with my uncoordinated, nerdy little sister for that long and I didn't know?" He's laughing as he asks, but I don't trust that it'll stick.

"Yes," I say, waiting for him to get pissed. His laughter slows, but he still has a smile on his face.

"Am I that unobservant?" he asks.

"I never acted on it until the summer before I went pro. I never even so much as held her hand." I tell him in a rush. I'm not looking for forgiveness. I wouldn't ask for that seeing as I don't feel bad at all about the way I feel about Winnie. I do want to explain to him though that I never meant to lie to him. "She cut things off after that and nothing has happened between us until I moved back to town." He nods, processing.

"Why didn't you ever say anything?"

"I wanted to eight years ago, but she told me she wasn't looking for something long term so she didn't want you to know, when I pressed her about it she broke things off and then pretty soon after that she broke off most of our communication."

"You know I thought there might be something between you a few years ago. She came back from a trip for school the same weekend you had a game in the city and was devastated. I couldn't get her to talk about it."

"A misunderstanding. Lacey was involved." I cringe remembering the texts on Winnie's phone.

"Uhg. Lacey. She was the worst."

"She was. More than I even knew. I'm wishing I would have listened to you about her sooner," I admit.

"So, you and Winnie? Are you together then?" I feel my heart sink, because I don't know where we stand at the moment.

"Well we were. I was planning on telling you about us the day of the accident, but Winnie has barely spoken to me since. I'm worried I might lose her."

"What did you do?" It's not exactly accusing, but his tone definitely says he thinks I've wronged his sister.

"Honestly, Colt, I didn't do anything. I think she's gotten in her own head and she won't let me in. She had a really hard time when you got hurt." He flinches at that.

"I didn't mean to worry her."

"I'm not saying anything is your fault. I just don't think she let's everyone see how hard it is for her. She takes care of everyone else and shoulders her own burdens all alone."

"She's never said anything." I love Colt, but sometimes he can be really selfish.

"She shouldn't have to." His eyes flick back to mine and seem to harden.

"She's my sister, Rhett. I would do anything she asked me to."

"I know you're a good brother and since you are you would know that she would never ask. She hates being a burden. She would rather suffer alone than to have someone know she was struggling." He just stares at me. I once again get ready to defend myself without hurting him.

"You're right," he says begrudgingly, surprising me. "I should have known she was struggling." He swallows and then continues. "You really love her? You'll treat her the way she deserves?" This is the easiest question I've answered so far.

"I love her more than I could ever put into words, but I'll still find a way to tell her how much she means to me everyday if she'll let me."

"Okay."

"Okay?"

"You may not have been looking for my permission, but since we've been kids we're all each other has had. It falls to me to look out for her. You're a good man, Rhett. My best friend and I love you like a brother, but if you ever do anything to harm her in any way, I will put you on your ass and make it hard for you to ever get back up." This was expected and I accept his threat with as much swallowed pride as I can. I nod my head.

"I won't, but if I ever do I'll be coming to you to straighten me out anyway."

"Sounds about right. Now, how are you gonna get her back?" I smile.

"I have half a plan—half a plan and a lot of determination." He laughs at that.

"That's all we've ever needed. I wish you luck. She's so damn stubborn."

"When it comes to Winnie I'm up for the challenge. Always."

WINNIE

I'm here at the bakery late again tonight. I've been here as much as possible the last week. I haven't spoken to Rhett in six days. His first game is tonight and I want to be there for him so badly. I feel like my body is caving in on itself. After recovering from my panic attack last week I had to come to terms with the fact that I am not strong enough to survive losing him. Also, for the first time since the night of their deaths I let myself be selfish and have something I really wanted. Only for my brother to wind up in the hospital with a head injury the next day. I'm not meant to have all the things I want. I had been selfish the night of my parents' accident, too.

The loss of my parents affected me in ways I'm still finding out about. I've been to therapy on and off over the years. There's obviously a lot more I'll need to work through, but losing them when I did, how I did. I know Colt was devastated by their deaths as well. We had fantastic parents. The best. They were fun and colorful. They loved us and they loved each other and that was evident. The night of their accident I had been such a brat. I physically flinch thinking about it.

They were on their way home from their weekly date like normal when they called home to check on us. I was pouting, because I wanted to go to Bailey Holt's slumber party that night and my parents had said no. I told them that I might feel better if they brought us home ice cream sundae supplies. My father had laughed when my mom relayed my request, a deep belly laugh that I can hear in my ears now. She had a smile in her voice as she told me they would be home, with the supplies, in 15 minutes.

When 15 minutes turned to 30, we didn't think too much of it. When 30 minutes turned to an hour, we heard a knock on the door and rushed to greet them. It had been Aunt Carol, telling us we needed to come to the hospital. We were told my father died on impact, but my mother suffered for 27 minutes before she died on an operating table. I let out a sob at the memory. Colt had been so strong and stoic. I was a blubbering inconsolable mess. It had been my fault. They were turning out of the grocery store's parking lot and a driver ran a red light while driving 60 mph, 25 mph faster than the speed limit. When my Aunt asked about the other driver they told us he passed on the ambulance ride to the hospital.

I thought hearing that the man who did this to us was dead would somehow make me feel better, but it didn't. It just felt like more death on my hands. Rationally, I can tell myself that the accident wasn't my fault and that it was just a tragic accident. But deep down in the pit of my consciousness, it still feels like I caused it. I'm not sure how to make that go away. When good things happen to me or I get what I want, I think it will always be tarnished by the guilty feeling that accompanies it. I don't want to saddle someone else with that burden or expose myself in that way to someone just for them to leave.

I'm leaning into my anxiety when the door to my kitchen swings open and I see Mary standing there. I want to cry at the sight of her. She's good at popping up when I need her. I think Rhett inherited that from her. His name is a stab in my heart. Her next question loosens the dam I've been building to keep my tears at bay for the last six days.

"Winnie, honey. What's the matter?" I break.

I tell her everything. That I'm in love with her son and I believe he loves me too, but I don't think I can take that chance with someone. Anyone. I tell her how I feel guilty when things work out for me and that I'm scared something bad will happen if I'm happy. I end my tangent with the fact that Rhett has left before and he could again. I may not be worth the trouble. She smiles sadly at me.

"I'm pretty certain Rhett thinks you're worth it, Winnie."

"Has he said something to you?" I sniff.

"You could say that." I raise my brow at her. "Here." She hands me the local paper, I am more confused now.

"Um thanks? I'll save the crossword for later."

"Not the crossword, Winnie. The sports column." I flip it over and see a picture of a smiling Rhett. God, he's beautiful. Below the picture the article's headline reads.

SILVERTHORNE ALUMNI, RHETT HOLLOWAY, TO LEAD BOYS HOCKEY TEAM TO VICTORY

"This is great, Mary. I really am so happy for him." I go to set the paper down and she sighs heavily.

"Read the article, Winnie. Please. Specifically the last few paragraphs." I eye her warily but concede.

When asked about being back in Silverthorne, Coach Holloway said as much as he is looking forward to coaching his team to victory, the biggest reason he sees himself sticking around here is that he's in love with the woman who owns the local bakery.

I gasp and tears fill my eyes as I keep reading.

"I love hockey and always will. Playing professionally for the past decade of my life has been a great privilege, but Coaching these boys the past few months has been the most challenging and rewarding. I'm hoping this season and in the years to come, I can prove to this community that I'm willing to put in the work to get these boys the opportunities they deserve. I'm planning on being around for a long while, if anyone had any doubts. There's a woman here that I've been in love with since I was seventeen and I plan to marry her as soon as I can get her to say yes... You may know her as the woman who runs and owns the very successful bakery, Thistle and Sage. They have the best cinnamon rolls in the state—"

I stop reading when the tears become too much for me to see through and wipe my eyes on the sleeve of my tee shirt. I let out a sob at the realization that I could have lost Rhett, because of my own stupidity. He wants me. He'll stay. I just have to take this small risk and the reward it will bring will absolutely outweigh it. I check my phone. Another unanswered message from Rhett time stamped at 3:37 this afternoon.

"I won't give up on us Winnie. You and me are end game. If you decide to take the risk with me, meet me on the ice tonight. I love you. Get in your head about it if you have to, but please take me with you."

I feel my lips tremble, clear my throat and glance at the woman who has been like a mother to me when I needed one the most.

"Can I still make the game?" Mary checks her watch.

"You have 15 minutes. If you hurry I think you can make it." I jump off the stool and sprint out of the front glass door and down the sidewalk to the school. I trip twice on the way, but only fall once, skinning my knee and scuffing my hands up. All I can think about is getting to Rhett. He needs to know that I'm all in like he is. That I will stick by him like he's promised to do for me. I need to tell him I'm so stupidly in love with him that I'll fight through all my insecurities to make us work.

I make it to the school in 10 minutes despite my clumsiness. It's the last two minutes in the last period when I burst through the side door of the arena. I spot Rhett immediately on entrance. He's in a suit and looking so devastatingly handsome that I can barely stand it. How could I have been so stupid? He's talking to one of his players before sending him out onto the ice. When I check the score board again I see how close the game is. 3-4. We're up by 1. I know how badly he wants this win. I bite my nail and shift from foot to foot. The time is running out and I'm vibrating with nerves. I want this for him.

When the buzzer sounds and we're still up by one I let out a whistle, cheering loudly. Rhett's celebrating with his team, but when they all head off to the locker room his eyes find mine instantly. I smile a watery smile. Pride inflates my chest for him. He's proven not only that he's the best player to ever step out onto the ice here, but that he's also going to be the best coach. His smile is wide, showing off his straight white teeth that he somehow managed to keep intact. I decide to make a run for him. Not my best decision. I jump the half wall on my end of the rink and try to run towards him. I feel my mistake as soon as my feet hit the ice, sliding until I'm falling. I land on my right hip and elbow.

He's there in a heartbeat, lifting me into his arms and carrying me to center ice. As painful as it is to hit the ice like I have many times before, being carried around in Rhett's strong muscular arms may be worth it.

RHETT

I've just coached my team to our first victory and I couldn't be more proud. These boys have put in the work and listened to everything I told them to do. I'm just missing one thing or I guess one person. So, when I look out into the crowd and see her standing next to the rink, I can't stop the smile that takes over my face. Before I can get to her she's climbing over the wall

Winnie Parker will never stop taking my breath away. She looks so beautiful it hurts. Her hair is as wild as I've ever seen it and her cheeks are pink. She's beaming at me and I stand a little taller knowing she's looking at me. I grin at her, but make a mad dash to get to her when she tries to move on the ice and falls onto her side. I'm worried she's hurt herself when I get to her side. I pick her up and walk her back to the center of the rink.

"You know, I wanted you to fall for me, but I really didn't mean physically. Are you alright?"

"I'm fine. I'm sorry, you know I can't walk on flat ground

without tripping, let alone ice." I chuckle. The weight I've been carrying in my chest lifted.

"I was starting to think you weren't coming and I was going to have to make a special visit next door."

"I wasn't. I had all but convinced myself that you were better off without me and I should let you go." I blink.

"As far from the truth as that is, I have to ask. What changed your mind?"

"I don't think I believe anything differently now. You probably are better off without me and you could have found someone else who is less trouble. Someone easier, but I wouldn't be better off without you, I'm not sure I could survive it again." She lets out a sob and I wipe the tears from her beautiful face. She has no idea the hold she has on me and before I can tell her that, she continues. "I'm so out of my mind in love with you Rhett. I'm so sorry it took me this long to come to terms with it." She's crying in earnest now, but I can't help my smile. Knowing she cares for me a fraction of what I feel for her has me feeling like I'm floating. I set her down on her feet, holding onto her by her forearms.

"Don't cry, honeybee," I whisper. "If it helps to know, I was never really that worried." It's a lie, because I had thought about how impossible it would be to not have her be mine, but I'm trying to be reassuring. "I let you go once before and I spent eight years missing you. I won't ever be that stupid again," I say, tucking her hair behind her ear.

"That makes one of us. I'm still so scared. I don't want to lose you, Rhett. It would kill me to lose you, but never having you because of a what if? That thought terrifies me." I take her face in my hands then, kissing her lips softly in the middle of the hockey rink, in front of the whole town.

"Never going to happen. I am yours, Winnie. Whatever parts of yourself you'll give me will be more than enough for me." She whimpers and reaches up on her tip toes, kissing me before pulling back.

"Rhett."

"Yes, Winnie?"

"I'm not sure if you realized, but I got your message." I grin wider.

"I was hoping you would. You should know I talked to your brother before I did the interview."

"You talked to Colt? How did that go?" she asks, sounding as if she thinks it went badly.

"It may take some getting used to, but it's all out in the open now. We're out in the open. I don't want you to ever doubt I'm in this for good, Darlin'." I breathe out the words in a rush.

"I love you," She says and I feel like my heart might beat out of my chest. "More than I thought I could love someone or anything. I will never stop loving you."

"I'm so in love with you I can't think straight, honeybee." She smiles at that

"I want you to know that I'm in this. I want you and even though I have a lot to overcome I want to trust that you will be by my side."

"I'll be there every step of the way. I don't want you to do this on your own. Not when you have me now."

"I know that. I want to lean on you, even though that's hard for me," she admits and I'm flying. All I want in this world is for Winnie to know she can rely on me.

"I want you. I will choose you. I won't let you fight these battles alone. All that I am is yours. I'm yours."

"And I'm yours."

I pick her up once more so she's wrapped around my waist and kiss her for all I'm worth. There have been times in my life where not weighing the odds got me into trouble—sometimes it even got me hurt. I've never been one to play it safe, but I always calculate the probability of success. Having Winnie though. Making her mine. Sharing a life with her. There has never been a doubt in my mind that she was worth the risk.

RHETT

I'm walking into my family home. Today is Thanksgiving and the start of a short break from hockey. Winnie has been busy with the bakery for the last month gearing up for the holiday. I finally convinced her to move in with me a couple weeks ago. We're keeping the cottage for now and making whatever renovations she wants to. I'm just happy to be included. Mostly it's for manual labor and for some reason she's always spilling things on my shirts, so I have to remove them.

The thought makes me smile even as my heart is beating out of my chest. Over the past month Winnie and I's relationship has become unshakable. She's trusting me in ways that I had only hoped for. Moving in was a big step, but I'm ready for something even more permanent. My palms are sweaty and the small box in my pocket feels like it weighs a thousand pounds as I walk into the kitchen where she's finishing up a crust for pumpkin pie, a pie I requested. She's so good to me.

I'm not nervous about asking Winnie to marry me. I've wanted to spend the rest of my life with this woman since I was

23 years old. I know there's no one out there that sets my world ablaze like she does. I'm only nervous she'll think I'm pushing her too much too soon. I don't want to scare her off, but I do want to call her my wife more than I have ever wanted anything in this life or the next. Well, only one way to find out. It's now or never.

"Hey, honeybee." When she turns and I see the flour on her jaw and covering her hands I can't help but feel more at ease.

"Hi. How was your last day of practice before break?" I take two long strides and cover her mouth with mine, needing the contact to steady me for what I'm about to do.

"I could get used to this greeting," she says with a shy smile. I clear my throat.

"Winnie?" She giggles.

"Yes, I'll make out with you, but let me wash my hands and honestly maybe your parents kitchen isn't the best place for this, then again...." She wiggles her eyebrows at me and I chuckle. I keep thinking I can't love her anymore that I do, but in one moment to the next that changes. I never want to be separated from her.

"That's not what I was asking, although I do want that to happen and I don't care if we're in the kitchen or the middle of the living room with my whole family watching." She snorts.

"Okay, well what did you want then? I need to clean up in here." She tries to turn for the sink but I take her hand in mine to stop her.

"Wha...?" She cuts off when I slowly lower myself to one knee, her eyes bigger than I've ever seen them.

"Winslow Parker, the absolute love of my life. I promise to stand with you in the storms that life brings, fight beside you when battles come to our door, and never let you feel like you are too much, only too good for me." A choked sob escapes her mouth and she places her flour covered hand over it, her honey eyes sparkling with unshed tears that I want to brush away, but I continue. "Darlin' will you let me take care of you and allow me this honor of calling you my wife?" I feel a hot tear slide down my own cheek, not having realized that I'm crying, too.

Winnie's hands slide down to my face and curl around the back of my head as she nods her own then finally utters the words I've been dying to hear. Ones I haven't been able to breathe until I hear.

"Yes, Rhett. I'll marry you. I'll make sure your huge, generous heart is safe with me." And there she goes again, making me love her more than I did just a minute ago.

THE END

ACKNOWLEDGMENTS

This has been an incredible journey. I have wanted to be a published author since I was thirteen years old and writing fictional entries into my journal. I have been a storyteller all my life so seeing one of my stories out in the wild is unbelievably humbling and surreal. I have an overwhelming sense of gratitude to anyone who played a part, no matter how small, in getting my book published. I won't forget it.

To my husband, Joe. Thank you for believing in me. For encouraging me to reach for dreams I had given up on or thought were unattainable. You make me bold and I will never stop being grateful for that.

To my parents, thank you for teaching me at a young age that hard work is rewarded and striving to do my best is worth it in the end.

I love you all and will forever be thankful for your support in all that I do.

Thank you,
XO, Bea

About This Author

Bea Borges is an Indie Author living out her dreams of a small town life in The Ozark Mountains.

She is married to her best friend and has two truly magical children.

She enjoys trash tv, baking treats, and hosting friends. Most days you'll find her reading a love story or possibly writing one, but if not, she's probably hiking.

She writes love stories about flawed people who are incredibly deserving of love.

Follow her on Instagram to see new books she's writing and also parts of her life she's sharing.

@beaborges.author

Made in the USA
Middletown, DE
12 May 2024